THE Panty THIEF

THE PANTY THIEF

NAOMI SPRINGTHORP

The Panty Thief

Copyright © 2023 Naomi Springthorp

Published by Naomi Springthorp

Print Edition ISBN 978-1-949243-54-3

The Panty Thief is a work of fiction and does not in any way advocate irresponsible behavior. This book contains content that is not suitable for readers 17 and under. Please store your files where they cannot be accessed by minors.

Graphic Designer: Irene Johnson

Editor: Katrina Fair

For the sister I chose…

CHAPTER ONE

RAYE

When did it become a fucking obstacle course to get to my room? I think to myself as I shut the door to my bedroom as silently as an electric car creeping through a parking lot. I went into stealth mode as soon as I pulled in front of the house and found the lights on. It's 3:30 in the morning and a newborn lives in the house, lights on is not a good sign. I slipped out of my high heels to eliminate clatter before I opened the door of my Audi. I unlocked the front door, entered and closed it behind me softly while holding the knob to avoid a loud click. Holding my crossbody bag with the chain strap close to my body so it won't rattle, I pad through the kitchen to my side of the house. I gaze across the living room to satisfy my nosey ass and catch a glimpse of my best friend in the whole world, Ashley, walking back and forth in the hallway bouncing baby Mac. Her man, Jonah, is sleeping like a baby, hot as fuck, and not a stress line to be seen. I'm surprised to find him sleeping, he's usually better than that. I slide into my room undetected, close the door, and change into my oversized Matchbox Twenty concert shirt.

All I want to do is sleep. I've been awake for over twenty-four hours and should've came home when the club closed instead of going to Maddux's for our own personal after party. I should've skipped the club too, but I can never resist an opportunity to sparkle up for the dogs on the dance floor. Unlike some of the other party girls, I've learned to arrive late and walk in like the beauty they've been waiting for all their lives. They see me for what I am—a perfectly put together thirty-something with the body of a twenty-something and bodacious curves to die for—and flock to me like moths to a flame. What can I say? I shine bright like a diamond.

Finally, I slide between my sheets and rest my head on my silk covered pillows. I close my eyes already anticipating sleep. All I can hear is Ashe trying to get Mac to go to sleep. Begging him to go back to sleep. She runs through everything she's done and I listen, "Mac, please! I changed your diaper. I fed you. I bounced you around. I took you for a drive. I fed you again. Mommy loves you, but I need sleep my little nut." In response he cries louder.

I can't sleep. I should go help her. She would help me, but I do everything possible to avoid getting knocked up and therefore don't have to deal with this situation. I couldn't sleep through the noise of their fornicating activities last night. This has got to stop or I'm going to get bags under my eyes and start looking my age. Damn, she must be tired with both of those boys wanting something all the time.

I turn on my soothing sounds app in an attempt to drown out the noise and get some sleep.

I gaze around my room, remembering all the good times I've had here with Ashe. I've only ever lived with my parents or her. It's like living with family because she's the sister I chose and I've had her in my life since grade school. We've had each other's back since then and no matter what that will never change. We painted this room together and talked the hottie who lives across the street into putting up the shelves around the room, a couple feet below the ceiling for me to put all my knick-knacks and stuffies on together. We've always gotten things done one way or another. Though my inner party girl has always been willing to offer more than Ashe, which is kind of funny, but not funny considering the current situation.

It's 4:15am and the house is finally quiet. I take a deep breath and….

I SHOOT UP STRAIGHT, "FUCK!" An alarm is sounding in the other room and it's 5am. Suddenly Mac is crying again.

This isn't working anymore. I need my own place. If I don't get some sleep soon, I'm going to lose my shit.

I throw the blankets off of me, pull on some leggings, tie my shirt in a knot in the front, pack a bag, and beeline for the front door.

Jonah's on a work call and Ashe calls after me, "Where are you going?"

"Somewhere I can sleep," I reply curtly.

"Can I go, too?" She asks.

"I'm going to Maddux's."

"Never mind."

I close the door behind me and observe the sun beginning to rise. The overcast morning causes it to be tinged an ominous dark red until the sun comes into view. I sit watching it from my car as I argue with myself, *Do I really want to go to*

3

Maddux's? The answer is I really want sleep. I'll figure out the rest later.

I PULL up in front of his place and stare at it. He owns a huge two-story home about a block from the beach and has a beach view from his master bedroom. When I say huge, I mean huge, and he's not compensating. I think it's got six bedrooms and eight bathrooms. The master bedroom has two bathrooms, a his and a hers. It's more of an estate than it is a house, with the pool and hot tub surrounded by the gazebo and outdoor kitchen in the backyard, and the six-car garage. I could live here and he wouldn't even know I was here.

This is a bad idea. I don't want to get attached to him like I was when Ashe started to date Jonah. I didn't even realize she was dating anyone I was so obsessed with Maddux. He is simply a well-hung sugar daddy. He is not the one. He's fun and he pays, but he's a dog. And men, heh, you know that once a dog always a dog. That's fine. They could say the same about me, I don't take offense. I live my life my way and have fun. Don't get me wrong, I'm a party girl not a working girl.

I guess it wouldn't be right to find an unlocked window and make myself at home without announcing my presence. Maybe he'd let me rent a room for a short time until I can find a place. At this point, all that matters is I get some sleep.

I grab my bag and walk up to his door. The home is suddenly larger than I remember and somehow looming over me and judging me for what I'm about to do when I left here two hours ago after over an hour of satisfying uninhibited sex. If the walls could talk, the gossip would all be about me. The things I do with that man. I was so into him that I'd do anything, and he was the best ever. I'd allowed the blinders to impact my opinion. He's satisfying, but I'm not giving him any more kudos than that.

With that, I ring the bell and chimes echo through his home.

CHAPTER TWO

RAYE

a sleepy Maddux opens the door wearing a burgundy silk robe. Every hair in its place. A satisfied swagger to his step, he gazes upon me like a piece of candy that he wants more of and who could blame him?

"Back so soon?" He does a retake on my appearance, "Is everything okay?"

"I need sleep. I can't sleep at home with the noise. Would you mind if I crash here tonight?" I wish the words hadn't left my lips and wonder how he'll respond at the same time.

"Of course. Stay as long as you'd like," he offers graciously.

"Are you sure? I'm going to start searching for a new place today. It's just not working anymore." I consider my words, not wanting to end up indebted to him, "Maybe I can rent a bedroom from you for a week or two?"

"Don't be a silly girl. You'll stay with me in the master suite."

He takes my hand and leads me directly there. I'm not up for another round. I can't keep my eyes open.

I toss my bag in the corner and gaze out at the ocean with the sunrise highlighting its cresting waves. It's mesmerizing, more so in my exhausted state.

"Come on, baby. Get in bed," he calls to me as he holds the blanket open for me.

It's as if the bed was calling me, not him. I go to its high thread count sheets and silk pillow cases on command, and enjoy the luxurious plush blanket as I get cozy with it pulled up around my neck.

I WAKE up surprised to find myself in Maddux's bed. I'm rested and recall last night as I clear my groggy head. He's not in bed and there's no water running in either of the master bathrooms. I get up and grab my bag, digging through it to find my phone. It's already the middle of the afternoon. I must have fallen asleep instantly, I didn't take any clothes off or even untie my shirt.

I check my phone and find texts:

Maddux: Good morning. You fell asleep on me last night.
Maddux: I have to handle some business today, so I'm at the office.
Maddux: Please make yourself at home. I hope you are there when I get back. <3

I'm startled by a soft knock on the bedroom door and watch it slowly open wondering who the hell is here and quickly roll off the side of the bed. Blankets and all wrap around me as I fall and quickly maneuver under the bed, squeezing my ass in with me. Suddenly wishing I had the ability to suck in my ass like I can my stomach. I've only been at Maddux's late at night. For all I know he may have a room-mate or a girlfriend with a key or a wife who's supposed to be on a trip somewhere. I could be the one who doesn't belong, or it could be one of those home invasions and I may be about to get tied up (not in a good way) or be the next victim of a serial killer.

A kind-hearted feminine voice speaks, "Hello? I have a delivery for Raye?"

The voice is obviously as confused as I am. At least it's a female, so I can probably take her. A delivery for me? Here? This could be a trap. How does she know my name? I stay silent and try to get a glimpse of her from under the bed. Sneakers on small feet, topped by black pants. I attempt to squirm to a better vantage point and my leggings audibly rip from the pressure between my ass and the bed frame slats. Last thing I need right now is a splinter in my ass on top of poten-tially being kidnapped and held for ransom.

"I can fix that for you. If you'd like," the kind voice offers.

"Who are you?" I inquire quietly.

"Mr. Quijada's housekeeper. You may call me Marta."

I instantly bang my head on the bed and yell, "Shit!" I groan and crawl out from under the bed the way I went in. Eventually managing to pop up off the ground with a smile on my face, pretending to have a shred of dignity, "Oh, nice to meet you. I didn't know he had a housekeeper."

"I know you. You're never here during my work hours," she says.

I remember why she was here, "Did you say there's a delivery for me?"

"Yes, ma'am. I have it downstairs. It's beautiful. Where would you like it?"

I stare at her, unresponsive.

"I have coffee ready downstairs. Please join me. I have a key for you per Mr. Quijada's request as well. I'm guessing you'll be staying for a while?"

"Hopefully not too long."

She cocks her head inquisitively, "You're in a relationship with him, no?"

A relationship? Hmmm. "I suppose, but this is just temporary. Our relationship is mostly during your off hours."

Her eyes get big, "Okay, I'll see you downstairs."

Shit. I quickly get dressed and as I step out of the master suite I'm overwhelmed by the smell of flowers. It's like stepping into a field of wild flowers. I walk down the stairs and find a huge floral arrangement filling the four-foot round entry table. A white envelope sticks up out of the pink and purple flowers, I take it and read the card...

Raye,
I hope these brighten your day like you brighten mine.
Maddux

I turn toward the kitchen and meet Marta at the coffee maker. The kitchen shines with high-end stainless-steel appliances, chrome backsplash, black granite counter tops, white marble tile, dark wood cabinetry, chrome chandelier-style lighting, and light reflections bouncing off everything. Modern and masculine, just like Maddux. She pours me a cup of coffee and hands me a keyring with a key and fob on it, "The fob opens the gate near the garage, so you don't need to park on the street. Don't park in front of the garage or you will block Mr. Quijada's vehicle from getting out of the garage. The key is just back up in case there's a breakdown in the system, it works on everything outside for entry to the property. The front door has a key code system on it and I've programmed the code '777*69' for you per Mr. Quijada's request."

I stare at her wide-eyed, "You really take care of this place, don't you?"

"It's my job to take care of Mr. Quijada," she states and continues, "and he takes care of me."

"Well, I don't intend to cause you any extra work," I say and think about the stains we've left on the sheets with the lubes we've used. This woman has probably cleaned my skid marks.

HE'S DRIVING ME CRAZY. Yes I appreciate that I can sleep and how he pays for things and that I have a roof over my head. The last more than you might be able to understand after searching for a new place to live for over a week unsuccessfully. I've been sparkled up and ready to go out three times this week to get a "Baby? Where are you going? Don't you want to stay here with me? I've got Marta cooking us chateaubriand with roasted baby carrots and garlic smashed red potatoes for dinner, and I think I smell her homemade yeast rolls in the oven (or something similar). What's the point of going out to the club when we are already here together?" Well, if I don't go my ass and other parts of me will get bigger, but I can't tell him that. The truth is that I love the club. Everything about it from the music and dancing to the wide selection of men and beverages. It's my zone. If I'm there, I'm queen and the rest can bow down to me. At least I imagine the fanfare and light focusing on me when I step through the door making my fashionably late entrance. I don't mind going with him, though I prefer to go alone. But he wants to stay home like an old married couple. That's not me. What am I supposed to do when he's been so hospitable? I change into something comfortable and join him in the theater room for dinner and a movie. (Yes, I said theatre room—it seats 20.)

CHAPTER THREE

TRUCK

"*V*in, what's going on with the empty unit? I need you to get that place rented out," I say as I scratch the scruff on my chin.

Vin rolls his eyes at me and says in an authoritative voice, "First, you know I prefer Vincent. I have reminded you of this many times."

"Fine. Vincent, what's the status on the empty apartment unit?" I try again adding a politer tone.

"It's pending." He glares at me, "I requested the giant, old school realtor-like sign you insist be installed out front a couple of weeks ago. Unfortunately, the owner is slacking. If you would let me put the vacancy online on one of the rental websites, it would already be rented."

"I don't want some creeper from the internet renting a unit in my building. You know the rule…" Vin cuts me off.

"We want to know what kind of vehicle they show up in. If they drive themself or get a ride. If it's well-kept or a hoopty

POS. We don't want them if they smell. They need to be a clean, non-smoker, with no holes in their clothes unless the holes are supposed to be there for fashion purposes. They need to have a smart phone so we can reach them when we need to send a message to the building. No flip flops because that's one step away from barefoot and you don't want anyone wandering the building barefoot." He rolls his eyes again and stares at me, "Foot freak."

"You don't want a murderer living in the building either. I think you enjoy the tenant selection process and I'm not a foot freak, they're just dirty."

Vin rolls his tongue in his cheek, "Dirty like the things you want to do to me? I'll go get a pedicure and clean them up for you, if that's your thing."

"You are a lovely man, but I don't swing that way," I say to Vin for the umpteen thousandth time since I met him.

He smiles at me, "It never hurts to try."

I pinch my eyes closed and open them, "Now, what about the sign?"

Vin shakes his head, "That requires digging a hole in dirt which would get my hands dirty. Getting my hands dirty is not included on my job description."

I glare at him blankly.

He hands me the key to the storage garage, "The sign is waiting for you."

I turn to go install the sign, "Remind me why I pay you."

"The owner of the building pays the manager to keep the building running smoothly. And in your case, to hide that you're the building owner from the tenants. I suppose we could just announce you're the owner in the next building text message."

"No. That won't be necessary." I remember the first building I bought and lived in, and how many nights I was woken up to fix leaky faucets, toilets that were overflowing, and unlock doors for tenants who couldn't keep track of keys. Luckily, Vin likes painting because I despise it and he found a cleaning crew to hire when units are vacated. This building is far superior—better location, more parking, twice as many units, and better cashflow. A property management company takes care of the original building and I learned my lesson. Don't tell anyone you own the building.

I make my way to the garage to get the task done. It's a warm day, so I pull my t-shirt off and hang it out the back of my surf trunks before I get to work. I love the warmth of the sun beating on my bare skin, it's one of the reasons I settled in OC. Nothing like the Southern California sun and sand. I could've chosen anywhere, but this place has always called to me.

I dig the hole and get the sign planted. It really is an eyesore, but I chose it on purpose. I want it to be seen. I need to keep the building rented out at 100%, so I can work on purchasing another building.

"Nice tan baby. Turn around and show us those abs," a convertible full of women yell at me as they drive by. Which reminds me of the other lesson I learned at the first building: Don't hit it in the building. In fact, don't flirt with it, don't buy it coffee, don't even gaze at it out of the corner of my eye. Keep women I'm interested in off the property completely. No exceptions, not even for one-night stands. Shit, especially not one-night stands. No crazy hos in the building, not as tenants or visitors or hook-ups of any kind.

I STOP in Vin's office on my way to my apartment after getting the sign in place, "Sign has been installed."

"I assumed so. I've had three calls already and have the

first applicant scheduled for her interview," he checks me from head to foot. "Is that how you presented yourself to the world as this building's maintenance man?"

"Is there a problem?" I glare at him wondering if he has forgotten who signs his paycheck and provides him with his apartment.

"No Sir. Not a single one. MMM, mmm, mmm!" Vin grins deviously.

"I'm sorry?" I side-eye him.

"The women who are applying have obviously seen you shirtless out there showing the world your gorgeous self," Vin says with attitude.

"Is that a problem?" I ask.

"Nope. I'm raising the rent," he giggles.

"I don't dislike the idea of more money, but what's your motivation?"

"Well, everyone knows you pay extra for a view," he states as a clear-cut fact.

"But..."

"I'm going to have to come up with more jobs for you to do shirtless," he grins.

"I'm not the attraction here. Rent the apartments. Stop trying to hook me up." I hope he's listening to me.

"Maybe take some photos for future reference to use for marketing," he continues with his smart-ass ideas.

I turn and leave his office before he comes up with something else for me to do.

CHAPTER FOUR

RAYE

I've been at Maddux's for a week when the call I've been expecting rings on my phone. "I'd ask if you're ever coming back, but I know you've been home," Ashe starts the conversation without a hello. Never a good sign.

"I picked up some clothes and necessities. You don't need me there. You have a family now. I'm in the way and my lifestyle doesn't fit," I stop and take a quick breath. "But I still love you and you'll always be my sister from another mister." A smile sounds in my voice as I hope she understands.

"I don't like it, but I understand and I've been thinking about it," Ashe starts all business. I don't bother to speak, she'll do it for me. "Before we get to the business side of things, I want to work on our relationship."

"What do you mean? Our relationship is better than most married couples."

"It is, but like a married couple—all relationships need

work and maintenance. I need to schedule regular calls or dates or something to make sure we are good." She takes a deep breath, "I'm doing my best and I don't think it's good enough right now. Mac, Jonah, work, no me time. So, what's it going to be. I want phone calls and live dates scheduled."

"Are you sure this isn't the business part? It comes off as business to me."

"One hundred percent. This is important. Don't make fun of a woman nearing her wits end," I detect the honesty in her admission.

"Okay. What's the plan?" I ask fully aware she already has one and it's probably written down with a printed copy waiting for me.

"A call most days and a date at least once each week— coffee, lunch, happy hour. Whatever."

"You got it. But I think you need to add mani/pedi to the designated bestie time. You can double down on your time that way—me and your pampering."

"Ohhh…. Yes! And shopping."

"Done."

"Which brings us to the business part of this conversation. I think you should rent one of my properties."

"No."

"No?"

"No."

"Why not?"

"I don't want you to take care of me. I need to be on my own. I don't want business between us."

"I'm sure you can find a place and manage on your own. I'm just saying that I can make it easier. We can make sure you are in a good building with cheap rent."

"No."

"Fine. But, if you won't let me help you with a place, we're going to need to go shopping to furnish your new place."

"I have furniture."

"You only have bedroom furniture. You don't have anything for the kitchen."

"I can get what I need."

"I want to keep your bedroom furniture. It fits so nicely in that room and I don't want to move it and find something new. It's going to be the guest room and always ready for you. So, leave it and I'll buy you a new one."

"Ashe, you don't need to do this. My job is good and I can cover it. We both knew it was going to happen sooner or later. Eventually you were going to find a man and have a family."

"You've always expected to move out because *I* was the one who moved to the next step?"

"Of course."

"How were you so certain?"

"I'm a ho. You're not."

"We're going shopping and I'm buying you furniture," Ashe states firmly.

"I have to find a place first."

"Have you been looking?"

"Yes, but so far all the vacancies have signs of roaches or mice. Thanks for showing me the signs by the way." Just one of the many benefits of my bestie being a property mogul.

"No problem. Make sure to look for mold and water damage too. I don't want you sick from toxic crap in the walls."

"Yes, ma'am," I laugh.

THE NEXT DAY...

Ashley: How's the apartment hunt?

Raye: Nothing new today.

Ashley: I have a vacancy that would be perfect for you.

Raye: We already discussed this.

Ashley: Fine.

The day after that...

Raye: A man offered to let me move into his house. I get the whole house to myself except his bedroom.

Ashley: Do you want a roommate? How much?

Raye: Free, but I have to dump his bedpan twice a day.

Ashley: Pass

Raye: I don't know. It's a nice place.

Ashley: How nice?

Raye: It's a whole 1000 square feet and I get my own carport.

Ashley: Where's that eyeball emoji?

Raye: LOL

And the next day...

My phone rings, "Hey Ashe."

"What are you doing today?"

"I have appointments to view two apartments."

"Okay. Coffee or lunch today?"

"I wish, squeezing in the apartments on my break. I gotta run, I'll check in with you later."

"Good luck, bye!"

Later that day...

I send Ashe a text because I've learned not to call and wake up Mac.

Raye: Are you available?

Ashley: I'll call in a minute.

My phone rings, "Hey Ashe."

"How'd it go today? Anything promising?"

"Well the eclectic charming abode with country club amenities was one of those silver metal trailers parked in a trailer park." I laugh and continue, "The pool is nice, but the trailer couldn't handle my nightly action."

"Okay, and the other?"

"Older building with crawl space underneath it and it has obvious water damage issues."

"How'd you know?"

"I put my foot through the kitchen floor."

"Pass."

"I've got another one to check out tomorrow."

"Where at?"

"Over by the mall."

"Hard pass. That's too far away."

"I like the mall."

"I like the mall, too. It's still too far."

"You realize I'm the one living there, not you?"

"It's not convenient. I have a new vacancy just down the street, right off the harbor, with a view."

"No."

Two days later…

Ashley: I think you like living with Maddux.

Raye: I'm not going to lie. The bed is comfortable, it's quiet here, and Marta takes good care of us.

Ashley: Marta?

Raye: His maid.

Raye: But he's killing me. I haven't been to the club since I got here.

Ashley: What?!

Raye: He's cramping my style. Party girls don't do commitment.

Ashley: Right… Are you sure we aren't revisiting the Maddux Phase?

Raye: Oh no. I see him for what he is.

Ashley: What is he?

Raye: A sugar daddy with a big house who's nice to me and likes sex.

Ashley: With maid service I wouldn't be in a rush to move either. Can you send her to my place?

Raye: She's in a committed relationship with "Mr. Quijada."

Ashley: Okay let me know when you are ready to move to one of my rentals.

Raye: I'm not moving to one of your rentals.

Ashley: At least think about it.

Raye: I did.

Ashley: At least humor me.

Raye: I'll reconsider it, but I'm not going to change my mind.

Ashley: Bitch.

Raye: I know you are the best property manager on the face of the planet.

Ashley: Not the best, but my properties are the most well-kept.

The next day…

Work is crazy today. I haven't been able to sneak any time to search for an apartment. Shit, it was all I could do to manage to get out to pick up lunch. The last thing anybody wants is me hangry. Driving back to my office with my chocolate milk-shake straw in my mouth and dipping my salty French fries in it, (because I never have days like this where I'm forced to resort to fast food, so when I do I make the best of it) there's a group of women in a convertible hitting on a shirtless hottie like they are a bunch of neanderthal construction workers. He's magnificent with the light sheen of sweat on his tanned, muscular body. There's something about a man doing physical labor, wiping the sweat from his brow… when what he was working on comes into view. It's an omen. An ugly-ass realty sign that says, "Apartment for Rent." I drove around the block and prepared to get a photo of the sign with the phone number. Thank you crazy girls for bringing that man and his work to my attention.

I dial immediately and hope for a live person.

"Thanks for calling the Hard Wood Apartments, the home of your dreams. This is Vincent. How may I help you today?" An upbeat male voice answers succinctly.

"Well hello Vincent. I'm looking for an apartment and saw the sign in front of your building. Can you give me the deets?"

"Of course, but first, who am I speaking to and how many people will be living in the apartment?" He inquires.

"I'm Raye and I will be the only one living there."

"Perfect. We have only one unit available and it's our over-sized one-bedroom floor plan on the top floor of the building. It's approximately 785 square feet and has a fabulous walk-in closet in the master suite. The unit features a half bath in addition to the full bath in the ensuite. All top floor units have a balcony as well and this unit overlooks the pool. The owner of the property is dedicated to keeping good tenants and no riffraff, so I'll need to do an in-person interview with you. Any questions?"

"It sounds like I'd love it. What's the monthly rent and deposit?"

"This unit rents for $2,200 per month and the deposit will be determined by our interview. Does that work with your budget?"

"It's on the high side. I probably don't need the oversized floor plan, but I think I can make it work."

"I have tenant interviews available at 3pm today, 11am and 1pm tomorrow. Which will work for you?"

"I'd love to do it today, but I'm at work. I'll take 11am tomorrow, and don't give my apartment away to anyone else until after you've interviewed me," I decide to stick the work comment in there so they know I have a job and income. I wonder if I should sparkle for the interview.

"I won't. I've got a feeling you will fit right in here at the Hard Wood Apartments. I will see you in the morning, and please bring your ID. Have a good afternoon, Raye."

"Thank you, Vincent. You just took the stress out of my apartment hunt." I hang up and scoot back into the office.

Raye: Meeting with a property manager tomorrow at 11am. Building is promising from the outside.
Ashley: Does it have a harbor view? You should just move into one of my buildings.
Raye: We've been through this.
Ashley: Call me tomorrow. Good luck.
Raye: Love you bestie!
Ashley: Yeah, yeah… love you, too.

CHAPTER FIVE

RAYE

*S*omething is not right with me this morning. My stomach is all widgey. My palms are sweaty and it's absolutely disgusting. I've changed my clothes three times deciding what's appropriate for meeting with Vincent. I considered sparkling up like I'm going to the club since it always gets me attention, but I may not want to draw attention to the fact that I'm a party girl. He probably doesn't want men traipsing in and out of the building at all hours, though that won't happen—I always go to their place. Never bring guys home was one of the first things Ashe instilled in me and something that I can agree with. Maybe I should dress like I'm going to work. What am I most comfortable in? Which outfit is fun yet respectable?

After changing again, I put my slides on and head downstairs.

"You look nice today. Where are you off to?" Marta scares the bejeezers out of me.

"Thank you. I have an interview," I reply honestly without too many details.

"Well good luck," she smiles.

"Thank you," I rush out the door before she asks more questions.

I drive up to the apartment building and the "For Rent" sign is still up. I park and find the manager's office easily, knocking on Vincent's door a couple minutes before 11am. "Come in," he calls out.

I open the door with a confident smile on my face, "Hello, I'm Raye."

He glances at his phone, "Right on time. It's nice to meet you." He stands and offers his hand to shake.

I take his hand and shake firmly. He's a thin man wearing jeans and a button up shirt with the sleeves rolled up to his elbows. His dark brown-black hair is perfectly styled with sunglasses perched on top like a headband, he's got friendly eyes, and paint stains on his hands and arms. He examines me up and down as he shakes my hand.

"Please have a seat." He gestures to the chair in front of his desk and makes a note in the file that's open on his desk.

I do my best to be lady-like and not plop down into the chair. I attempt small talk, "How's your morning going so far today?"

"Good. I've had my coffee and there's a lovely woman sitting in front of me. Would you like some coffee?" He turns and points at the hot delicious smelling pot that's calling out to my soul.

"No thank you," I opt out mostly because I don't want to show him how talented I am at spilling it all over myself.

"Then let's get started. First thing on the list is a copy of your ID."

I fumble through my purse for my wallet, pull my driver's license out and hand it over to him. He gazes over at me and back down at my license. Holds my license up for a view of me and it at the same time. Takes a photo of my license, "Please stand up so I can take a picture of you." I must make a face because he continues, "You and your ID don't match. The owner will want to see the real thing."

"Does that matter? What I look like can make or break me getting the apartment?"

He stops and glares at me, his curved lips suddenly a straight line like a Peanuts character, "Not your personal features, but yes."

This is crazy. I stand and sling my purse over my shoulder ready to leave.

"I understand your trepidation," he stands and walks over to close the door. "You have nothing to worry about in this respect. Please understand, the owner is unique and takes very good care of the property and its tenants. This is one of the ways he attempts to keep our little community happy and safe."

"I'm sorry? You're going to have to elaborate," I change which foot my weight is on.

"The owner likes people who are clean and wear nice shoes for their interview." He leans in closer to me, "I like you. I think we will be great friends. Between you and I, I think he has a thing about feet—but I can't get him to show any interest in mine," Vincent scoffs.

I can't help but giggle, "Fine." I pose for him and make the best of it. He's harmless, but who knows how many photos of tenants the owner has plastered on the walls of his home.

Vincent continues working on his checklist, "I've got your phone number, email address, previous address... Your previous landlord gave you a shining review and was obviously sad you are moving. Just to confirm, you have no pets of any kind?"

"Correct, no pets."

"If that is going to change, please get pre-approval on the animal with me beforehand. Everything except a fishbowl that is three gallons or less. Do you have a vehicle?"

"Yes."

"Our parking spots are average sized and can be tight for a SUV. There are a handful of spots that are larger on the North side of the building, they tend to be the first filled and we ask that they be left for those with larger vehicles. What type of vehicle do you have?"

"It won't be a problem. I drive a sporty compact, an Audi TT." I wonder if Ashe is going to let me buy her hand me down again because it will probably be the last two-door she has. She leases vehicles and I've made a habit of buying out her leases when she's done. They are a few years old, well taken care of and much more affordable.

"That makes it easy. What are your hobbies?"

I stare at him dumbfounded.

"Do you cook or bake? Are you into art? Are you a musician? A bibliophile? An audiophile? Gym rat? Crafter? You must do something in your free time."

I'm in this deep, I might as well go for it. "I only cook because I'm hungry. The only music I play is on my air pods. I'm not a huge reader, but I love gossip magazines. I have no artistic skill, but I appreciate the art of others. Have you seen the size of my ass? Do you think I go to the gym?" I chuckle. "The only exercise I get is at the dance club."

"Who do you spend the most time with?"

"My bestie and I are inseparable. I'll be surprised if you don't hear from her before I can move in, that is if you accept my application and I'm still interested after this interrogation."

"How much do you want to pay for rent?"

"As little as possible," what kind of question is that! "I can afford the $2,200, but I was hoping to somehow magically keep it under $2,000."

"Keep in mind the rent here includes Wi-Fi, water, trash, gas, and cable. You will only have electricity to pay on your own. Do you have existing services you will be moving?"

I hadn't considered this. I'm going to have deposits. "No, everything is in my roommates name and she's keeping the place."

"Okay, well at least you will only have the deposit on the one utility." He reviews his checklist, "Do you have a boyfriend you may want to move in?"

"No," I may have answered too quickly. Maddux is the closest thing to a boyfriend I have and he'd never move here from his mansion with maid service.

"So, no boyfriend?"

"Not really. Haven't found one worth committing to."

"Me and you both, sister," he nods his head. "Who wants a deadbeat weighing them down?"

"Right? I want to have fun and enjoy life. Keep it light. Maybe someday I'll be surprised by Prince Charming's magic kiss, but it hasn't happened yet and I'm not holding my breath."

"I'm the king of kissing toads," he chuckles as he continues down his checklist. "It looks like I have everything I need from you. Do you have any questions for me?"

"When will I know if I get the apartment? Does it come with all the appliances?"

"It includes all appliances including washer and dryer. I have to meet with the owner to review your application, so it depends on his schedule—usually within 48 hours."

"Okay. You know how to reach me if you have any questions."

"I do. I must say, I have a friend that you would match perfectly with. You'd be a gorgeous couple," he smiles with matchmaking in his eyes.

"Let's not get crazy now," I laugh and rethink it. "But feel free to let me know if he's ever visiting so I can check him out."

"That's my girl. You never know who might be the one." He stands and opens the door, "Have a great afternoon."

I leave wondering if I just applied for an apartment or a dating service.

CHAPTER SIX

TRUCK

Vincent: I have an applicant to review with you.
Truck: Okay. Only one?
Vincent: Yes. We only need one.
Truck: I'd prefer a couple to choose from.
Vincent: You get one.
Truck: Again, I pay you.
Vincent: Yes. You pay me very well.
Vincent: When can you come down to the office?
Truck: I just got home from surfing. I need to shower
and I'd like a nap.
Vincent: Come down now.
Truck: Do you know what it's like to have sand stuck
to your nads?
Vincent: Then move quicker so you can get back to
shower.
Vincent: This will only take a few minutes.

I pull my t-shirt back over my head as I head out the door to the office. I'm wondering more and more who exactly is in charge around here—it isn't me.

I walk into the office and Vincent is dancing around nervously on his tip toes.

"She's the one!" He blurts out. "I mean, she's the perfect tenant," he says more calmly.

"Tell me about her."

"Well, her license says she's 5' 7" but that must've been on a goofy hair day. I'd say she's 5'6" if she's lucky. She's got eyes as green and as deep as the sea, and her hair is shoulder length strawberry blond spiral ringlet curls. She's absolutely adorable and curvy and feisty. Here, let me show you—"

"What do you mean show me?" I ask as I watch Vincent open his phone and go to his photos. "You did not..."

"Yes I did. I always take a photo of their ID for our file. Her ID doesn't do her justice so I took a few more." Vin stops and glares around the room, "She thinks I took one because her ID doesn't resemble her."

He turns his phone to show me and flips through at least a dozen photos that are all almost exactly the same. Vin's right, she gorgeous.

"Decline her application."

"What? She's the perfect tenant. She's got a small car. She's got the right income. No pets. No roommate. No boyfriend. No obvious baggage, just a bestie which means I won't have to be her therapist."

"You heard me. Decline her." I turn back and ask, "How do we know she doesn't have a boyfriend?"

"Oh, it's part of my interview questionnaire. Asking if there would be any potential roommates or boyfriends moving in."

"Stop. Stop right there. I don't want to know what else you

asked her that we aren't allowed to ask about. Are you trying to get us sued?"

"I would never get us sued. She's not that type. I know how to read people. I eliminate those types, we don't want them here."

"Good." I breathe hoping I can trust Vin's senses.

"Anyway, I told her $2,200. She'd like to be under $2,000," Vin continued.

"Why are we still talking about this woman? I told you to decline her."

"This woman's name is Raye and I like her. She might be good for you."

That's what I was afraid of. I'm not playing the dating game hosted by Vincent Ferrar again.

"Will you just look at her! How can you tell that face no?"

"Why'd you tell her $2,200?" I ask as an afterthought.

"I told you I was raising rent because of the view," he smirks.

"That's an increase of over 10%."

"Are you complaining? We run a great building here. Plus, the view of you shirtless got us over a dozen applicants."

I take his phone and swipe through the photos again. He's right, I can't tell that face no. "What do you want to offer her?"

"$2,000 per month with a two-year lease and I'll include all the things so we can evict her at any time."

"That's still more than what I require," I glare at Vin.

"She should have asked for lower rent. I aim to please, not give things away."

I pinch the bridge of my nose and close my eyes as I make a bad decision, "Go ahead and approve her. I can't win this with you."

Vin claps his hands excitedly, "Thank you! I'll have the cleaning crew through to do a last light cleaning and get her moved in within the week."

"Good job, Vin," he glares at me. "I mean Vincent. Is there anything else you need me for today?"

"I happen to have a chore for the hot maintenance man," he smiles. "The eye sore "For Rent" sign needs to be taken down and stored, and the hole it made needs to be filled to avoid someone tripping."

"Of course it does."

"Today, please. These calls about the vacancy are tiring and waste my time," Vin is suddenly all business.

"Yes Sir."

"Thank you."

CHAPTER SEVEN

RAYE

"*H*ello?"

"Hi, Raye! This is Vincent. I'm so happy to be calling you this afternoon to invite you to move into Hard Wood Apartments. We would love to have you as a tenant. The owner is allowing me to offer you the rate of $2,000 per month if you sign a two-year lease agreement that has stipulations allowing us to evict you if necessary."

"That's awesome, but why would you need to evict me?"

"I don't think we will, but you never know what can happen with people."

I nod to myself happy to save the $200 per month, "Sounds good to me. Thank you."

"I have keys and the agreement ready for you. I'm going to have the cleaning crew go back through it again before you move in. It should be ready in three or four days, will that work for you?"

"Yes, please!"

"Perfect, I'm going to email the agreement to you for your signature and I would appreciate it if you got that back to me within 24 hours."

"No problem. Thank you so much," my interior squeal squeaks out into the atmosphere. The email pops in and I complete the agreement before I do anything else.

Raye: I got the place!

Raye: I just signed the agreement!

Raye: I move in five days.

Raye: When are we going shopping?

Ashley: Did you read the agreement?

Ashley: I wish you would've sent it to me first for review.

Raye: I'm an adult. I can read. I've learned property management by osmosis.

Raye: How about "Congrats on the new place!"

Ashley: Oh! YAY!! I'm so happy you found a place! I can't wait to see it!

Raye: Better. Forced, but better.

Ashley: I'm on no sleep and Mac is sucking me dry. It's all I can muster.

Raye: Understood. When are we going shopping?

Raye: We should have lunch while we are out.

Raye: Maybe alcoholic beverages.

Ashley: Let me check with Mighty Midge and get time blocked on Jonah's schedule.

Raye: You schedule babysitting time with your man's assistant?

Ashley: It's great! I don't ask him for help. I just tell Midge what I need and she puts it on his schedule. No questions asked, it just happens and she doesn't schedule anything else for him during that time.

I stop and consider the scenario. There's no question he'd do it. I may need to chat with this Mighty Midge person.

Raye: We should schedule our dates.
Ashley: I was hoping to. We'll do that at lunch on our shopping day.

I PULL into Maddux's and park, making sure I'm not blocking the garage. Marta has made it clear that my previous parking job wasn't acceptable. I walk up to the front door with a bounce in my step and tap in my code. The door clicks and I push it open, closing it behind me to avoid yet another scolding from Marta. *"No slamming the door. Make sure it clicks closed. This is not a barn."* She's a small woman with a big bark. She doesn't like me. My guess is she wants "Mr. Quijada" all to herself. I wonder if that's why he's still single? Do you think she chases the women away? She's nothing compared to a screaming newborn and 5am alarms.

Maddux turns his attention from the stock market update he watches every weeknight, "Hey baby! Come sit with me. Tell me what's got you so happy this evening." He's all smiles and I can't wait to tell him.

I sit down next to him with my feet tucked under me and he instinctually wraps his arm around my shoulders. He gives me a sweet peck on the lips.

"I found an apartment. I move in a few days, so I will be out of your hair and no longer an inconvenience to your world."

"You're moving?" He asks as if that wasn't the first thing I said to him when I asked if I could stay a couple weeks while I apartment hunted.

"Yes."

"You should just stay here. That would be better."

"I need a place for me and my stuff. I've invaded your space long enough."

"Baby, you're anything but an invasion. Stay." He gets up, walking toward the kitchen and turns back to me, "That's settled."

Did he? He did not just make a life decision for me. I get up and follow him to the kitchen, "You're correct. It's settled. I'm moving." Marta gazes up at me from chopping vegetables and smiles giddily, probably happy I'm going.

He turns to me, "Why don't you want to stay?"

The intensity in his eyes tells me this is more to him and I've upset him. "I need my own place. I went straight from my parents to Ashe…"

"Who is like a parent," he interjects.

I grin and continue, "and I've never been on my own. I refused to rent from Ashe. I don't want special favors. I need to do it on my own. Rite of passage or something like that."

"Did I do something wrong?"

"No. Nothing is changing with us."

"Yes it is. You're moving out."

"This was temporary. You didn't ask me to move in with you. I'm not your girlfriend. I'm one of the party girls from the club. I can't be the only one. I've got to be cramping your style."

"Why would you say that? There's only you."

Oh fuck.

I can't go back.

"If you want more than a fuck buddy… our relationship can't start this way. I need to move and we can go from there."

"You're not moving."

Now he's pissing me off, "You just want a live-in fuck."

"That's not true! We're good together."

"The sex is good."

"You know what I meant. We're more than that, Raye."

"You like having sex living with you just like you have a maid taking care of you. At least you don't expect me to pick up after you." I stop and take a breath, "Do you realize we haven't been out since I got here? All we do is sit around watching TV and movies. That's not what I want. I love to go to the club and go dancing and just go out."

"Let's go out tonight." He turns to Marta, "Make dinner reservations for two for tonight and put away dinner for tomorrow's lunch, please." He turns back to me, "Get ready."

Asshole. I don't want to go out with him after this. I do want to go dancing. "You don't get to call all the shots. You can't just make reservations and think it makes everything better."

"Do you want to go out or not?"

"Yes." Damn it. The club always wins me over.

CHAPTER EIGHT

RAYE

*I*n my head it's a celebration dinner, not an asshole trying to take over my life and convince me to stay bribe. I'm not letting him ruin my night. I might not even go home with him. I talk to myself while I pick which of my club dresses to wear tonight. Tonight I'm going to sparkle more than normal. I slither into my gold and silver paillette sequined mini bodycon dress. I'm limited. I brought over a bunch of dresses in anticipation of nights at the club, but only a few pairs of shoes. Luckily this dress and my favorite black stilettos will be perfect together. I add some extra bounce to my hair, thicken my black eyeliner and add a few rhinestones like they are floating away from the outer edge of my eyes. I toss my lipstick, phone, and wallet into my small matching crossbody bag and make my way downstairs in search of Maddux. I'm good. Let's get this night going!

Halfway down the stairs, I'm all smiles when he gazes up at me, "I love you in that dress. Go change. It's inappropriate."

"What are you talking about? It's fabulous!"

"Not for the restaurant we have reservations at. They'll assume I've hired an escort."

I'm not sure if I should be offended or not. I suppose it depends on what level of escort he hires. "How often do you hire an escort? Do you hire the cheap one that looks all skanky or the higher end one that still has all of her teeth and good hair?" Sometimes I need to consider my audience. Remind me not to drink or eat anything Marta makes, she may poison me after this. Damn it—I love her coffee.

He stares at me, "I'm sorry, you will not speak to me that way in my home. Please go change into something more appropriate."

"Exactly, your home. I'm getting my own home."

"Raye, please change. I'm taking you out on a date, not just a quick meal and the club. I don't want to be late for our reservation. It's a very nice restaurant with live music and dancing. We're lucky to get a table on this short of notice," he pleads in a soft, sweet tone.

I stand there and stare at him, not wanting to change a thing. He did ask nicely, and I've never been to this place. I wouldn't want to be the only skank in the room. It's not like the club where the party girls rule the place. I center myself and go back to change.

I pull my black 3/4 length puff sleeve dress out with the deep sweetheart neckline, belted waist, and A-line skirt. I change dresses and keep everything else the same. He can't have a complaint about this dress.

With a little less pep in my step I get to the entry way, ready to go. I stand there waiting, taking a (good look) at his home around me. It's not me at all. It's formal. The master suite is on one side of the house, has its own staircase, while a grandiose stairway near the back of the home takes you to the other bedrooms. Old paintings of people I don't know with ornate frames hang on the walls. It doesn't fit him either. At least it doesn't fit my vision of him. Maybe I'm less acquainted with him than I thought.

He comes walking out of the kitchen wearing a stunning suit and tie, "Baby, you look beautiful. Perfect for our destination." He takes my hand and leads me out the front door to a limo where the driver has the car door open and waiting for us. I don't say a word. I'm along for the ride tonight. Though I'm not sure why we aren't taking his sports car.

Maddux slides into the car next to me and pops the cork on a bottle of champagne that's been chilling for us, pouring us each a flute. He scoots in closer and wraps his arm around me for the ride to the restaurant.

It seems like no time at all and we are stopped in front of the restaurant. The driver opens the door and Maddux gets out first so he can take my hand and assist me. The ground is a reflective mosaic of marble tiles and sea glass forming a crashing wave. I'm not wearing shoes for the slick and uneven entry, but I can dance in these so I can handle it.

We walk directly to the maître d' who welcomes Mr. Quijada by name and immediately leads us to our table in the shadows of the dance floor. "Will this table be acceptable, Mr. Quijada?"

"This is wonderful. Thank you."

"Would you like a menu this evening or are you ordering your usual?"

He better get a menu so I can order. He has a usual?

"Actually, whatever the chef's menu is tonight will be perfect for both of us. With the wine pairings please," he nods to dismiss the servant.

"I'll get your order submitted and have the sommelier bring you something to start with," he leaves the table on task.

"What did you order?" I ask.

"Whatever the chef's specialty is for the night."

"What is it?"

"I don't know. I didn't look at the menu."

"What if it's disgusting. Something we don't like? I would have liked to see the menu. I can order for myself."

"It's always an edible adventure, especially with the wine pairings."

"I'm not into wine. I'm more of a whisky or tequila girl. You know all of my 'J' men... Johnny, Jim, Jack, Jose, Jameson."

"It will be a great experience for you to try something different."

"I've tried it. I don't like it."

"You just haven't tried good wine and it's different with the meal pairing. You taste the wine. You taste the food. You taste the wine again to experience them alone and then the flavor that develops together."

"I understand the concept. I'm not an idiot. I'm not a wine girl."

"All I ask is that you try it tonight. For me. Please. You said we needed to go on dates. I'm trying to do that."

"I'd have been happy going to the club and the all-night diner. It doesn't need to be elaborate for me."

"Everything isn't for you. For some this is the norm. I enjoy it every week or so, but I'm typically by myself."

The sommelier stops at our table, "This is a little something to get you started tonight. I've arranged pairings to be brought to you with each course. Your meal this evening will be:

Starter: Brie Cheese En croute

Appetizer: Stuffed Jumbo Prawns wrapped in Bacon

Salad: Baby Green Salad with roasted Pear Skewers and Walnuts

Main Course: Pan Seared Duck with Spanish Beer Glaze

Dessert: Malasadas with Vanilla Anglaise and fresh berries

If you have any questions, please let one of us know. The chef is proud of tonight's menu and hopes you enjoy it."

I have a question, can I get a doggy bag to take most of it back to Marta? Can I skip the appetizer and the main course? Prawns are the bugs that eat all the shit off the ocean floor and I'm not about to eat a duck. I wish I'd brought a bigger purse.

I SURVIVED DINNER. I kept telling myself the club is in my near future, something to look forward to. The baked cheese was good. I faked an allergy to shellfish. The salad and roasted pears were delightful. The baby carrots and Brussel sprouts were tasty with the beer glaze. The deep-fried donut holes filled with goo—I'd like seconds. I tried each of the wines. By the time we got to the salad course, it didn't matter what it tasted like because I was buzzing. Overall it made the evening a lot more endurable. The food was gone. The club was next. Except...

Maddux stood and reached for my hand. I followed suit and grabbed my purse, ready to leave. "You can leave your purse," he says. "It's safe here."

I'm lost but continue to follow his lead.

He takes me to the dance floor and we dance to the live music. I'm comfortable at the club. This is something completely different. He has these skills, I don't. He leads and I follow the best I can. I have no idea what dances we were doing, but he changed the dance with each song and spun me like I was a part of him. Not necessarily the best idea after five glasses of wine and champagne while wearing stilettos. Maddux kept me from hitting the ground more than once, yet it didn't stop him from pretending I was a human top.

He leads me off the dance floor, "You're a fabulous dancer. We may need to get you some better dancing shoes."

"I have no clue what I was doing other than letting you lead and spinning," I giggle still buzzed.

"I had fun with you baby. You're right, we need to go out more often," he leans down and kisses me.

"Are we going to the club next or do you have other plans for this date?" I question teasingly, ready to get to the club.

We walk out to the car and as we are getting in he directs the driver, "Take us home please."

I pout, "No club?"

"Sorry baby, I have an early meeting in the morning. We'll go to the club soon," he kisses my forehead.

I wanted to go to the club. I get it, it's a weeknight and he's trying. Be patient, Raye.

CHAPTER NINE

RAYE

*W*hat did I learn last night? Wine gives me a hangover.

It's been a day that I'd like to forget. The piercing headache while I try to work and read off the computer monitors, and incessant high-pitched noises from the office equipment have me wanting to completely shut down and puke my guts out at the same time. My 'J' boys never do this to me, they respect me and I respect them. Maybe I should've respected the wine, but I don't have that type of relationship with all those different wines so I guess I'm paying for it.

I can't wait to get home and go to sleep.

Ashley: I gave Mighty Midge your schedule and your phone number.
Ashley: She's getting our dates scheduled.
Raye: You're using Jonah's assistant?
Ashley: She prefers it this way, it gives her more control of the schedule.
Raye: I suppose his schedule is fuller than yours.
Ashley: I don't know about that, but mine is more flexible.
Ashley: She's matching up his schedule with yours. She guaranteed me a shopping day in the next couple days.
Raye: Can Mighty Midge run my life too?
Raye: Does she know how to get rid of a hangover?
Ashley: No! You never get a hangover.
Raye: Nope… unless I drink wine.
Ashley: You don't drink wine.
Raye: Not by choice. He took me out to a fancy pants place with wine pairings.
Ashley: Do I want to know?
Raye: Five glasses of wine and champagne. Then dancing or I should say spinning.
Ashley: Go home and go to bed.
Raye: As soon as I'm off work…

My dark sunglasses blocked out the sun, letting me sleep in my car on my breaks and saving me from the potentially migraine causing sun. I love being out in the sunshine, I can't stand what wine did to my relationship with the sun.

It doesn't matter. I'm almost back to Maddux's palatial spread where I can go hide in a corner and sleep.

I park in the Marta approved spot, tap my number into the front door keypad, and listen for the click. I push the door open ready to find solitude and sleep.

The entry way table is set for two—champagne (oh fuck me) chilling in a beautiful crystal ice bucket with matching flutes waiting nearby, two tall taper candles are romantically lit and held high by shiny silver pedestals. The table is set with a black tablecloth, ivory cloth napkins, polished utensils, formal china, and a single long-stem red rose lying across one of the plates.

Maddux walks up all put together and in prime form, "Welcome home baby." He reaches for my hand, pulls me to him and kisses my cheek. "I thought we'd try something different tonight. I gave Marta the evening off and hired a personal chef. We had such a good time last night, I thought we should keep it going."

Please no more prawns, no more duck, no more strange food, and for goodness sake no more alcohol. Can we have a burger or macaroni and cheese maybe? French fries would be wonderful. Pizza sounds fantastic. I'd settle for a slice of bread and to be sent to bed for being a bad girl.

I smile attempting to make the best of it. It's too late to say not tonight. Then again, he didn't ask. It's what he wants, just like everything else.

He pulls the chair out for me and I sit, instantly greeted by the personal chef pouring champagne. Is this one of those scenarios where the hair of the dog who bit you can make it all better?

He takes a long draw on his champagne, swirling it around in his mouth, "Not too dry, not too sweet. It's absolutely perfect, just like you. Try it, tell me what you think."

"I appreciate what you've done here, but I'm still getting over last night," I scrunch my aching head and attempt a smile.

"Maybe just a sip, so we know for next time then?"

I raise the glass to my lips and the scent alone is enough to make my stomach roll. "I like the light bubbles, but I can't stomach a drop right now."

Happily interrupted by the personal chef, yet concerned about what he we was going to place in front of me at the same time.

He sets a plate in the center of the table, "This is our starter tonight, rustic bruschetta. I prepared a balsamic reduction as well as an herbed olive oil for dipping."

Bread. Exactly what I asked for. I pick a piece up and Maddux bumps his against mine, "Cheers." I take a bite and it's tasty and tangy, yet not so much that it angers my unsettled belly.

Something is up with Maddux. He's quiet tonight.

The chef returns with two salads, "This is Pea Salad with Pecorino, a light transition and palette cleanser between the bruschetta and the main course." He nods and walks away.

The plate is pretty with fresh peas, rosemary sourdough croutons, mint leaves, pea shoots, and large shavings of pecorino cheese, all dressed in a light vinaigrette. I dive in immediately. Apparently I'm hungry. I gaze up at Maddux, "I like this chef guy. Flavors right up my alley. Fresh, yummy, and nothing crazy." I focus on him, "Great idea."

His chest puffs out at the kudos, "I'm so happy you like it, baby."

We eat together silently until the chef shows up with the main course, "Sautéed chicken breast in a sun-dried tomato cream sauce with fresh basil, over angel hair pasta."

Pasta and chicken? I may love this chef. "It's beautiful colors."

"We eat with our eyes first," the chef replies. "I never forget that."

"Your dishes show it." I dig in and Maddux watches me eat, not touching his plate. He's been spoiling me and overall a gracious host. I'm going to miss his sugar daddy ways. Of course, I'll consider dating him if he truly wants a relationship with me. I'm not bringing up that I'm moving out.

"I've been thinking about what you said last night. I'm working on doing things, going out with you, things that you will enjoy and we can enjoy together. Be patient. I will figure it out. I'm accustomed to getting everything I want," he says like a planned speech he memorized.

"Thank you for taking me into consideration," I say between bites.

He visibly relaxes and takes another sip of champagne.

I'm about full and can't believe I've eaten as much as I have. I'm about ready to tap out when the chef returns again with dessert and the aroma of hot fudge reaches my nostrils. "For tonight's dessert, Hot Fudge Lava Cake with strawberries and fresh whipped cream."

Suddenly I have more room in my stomach. Maddux picks up a strawberry, drags it through the whipped cream and reaches across the table to offer me a bite. My fork is already slicing into the cake. I'm a happy girl and will need to start a new exercise routine tomorrow. He gets the cream on my nose and stands up with napkin in hand. He stops in front of me and pushes my hair behind my ear, "Baby, you are beautiful."

He kneels down and takes my hand, holding it gingerly while he fusses in his pocket with his other hand. I cock my head at him, "I have a napkin right here, you can use it to wipe the whipped cream off."

He caresses my cheek and pulls his hand out of his pocket with a small black velvet box, "Raye, will you marry me?" He flips the lid of the box open revealing a two-carat princess cut diamond solitaire set in platinum.

I pop-up out of my chair like a jack-in-the-box, "OMG!" "Pop Goes the Weasel" is on repeat in my head as if it was on demand.

"Is that a yes?"

"It absolutely is not. What do you think you're doing?"

"Proposing to the love of my life."

49

"We're not in that place. I'm moving out. We are maybe going to date. No. The answer is no," I step away from the table forfeiting the scrumptious chocolate dessert.

"You need to reconsider your answer immediately."

"No, I don't."

I run up the stairs to gather my things quickly with him yelling after me, "Raye! Get back down here."

I move quickly. It won't take long for him to follow me up here and I'm done with this. I grab as much as I can carry and pass him on his way up the stairs. "Raye! Stop! Let's talk about this."

"Why? You don't listen. I told you we needed to start with dating if you want a relationship with me."

"I took you out last night and dinner tonight…"

I cut him off, "That's not dating… it's not enough." I open the front door and hurry out, slamming it behind me. I pop the tiny trunk of my car and drop everything in it, get in my car and go home to where I belong with Ashe.

A few blocks away I turn onto a side street and pull over, sitting in my car strangling the steering wheel and cursing at the top of my lungs, "Asshole! Why couldn't he have done this when he was all I wanted?" I pound on my steering wheel and slam my head back against my seat repeatedly. "Fuck! I walked out on my sugar daddy!" Did he actually propose to me? That was the whole romantic dinner set up? What was he thinking? "I'm the 'love of his life'? Huh? He only thinks of himself." Did he propose to me so I wouldn't move out? "Asshole!" I lean my forehead on my steering wheel while I grip it tightly with both hands and close my eyes. I can't believe this is happening. I should've grabbed the dessert on my way out the door.

CHAPTER TEN

RAYE

I pull up at home and every single light in the place is on. Never a good sign.

I leave my stuff in the trunk and walk up to the house, already hearing a crying baby. I take a deep breath before I open the door. Ashe is right there and whips around to check the door. Her eyes wide, "Gracing us with your presence tonight?"

Apparently she's not having a good night either.

"I'm back here until I get moved in at the new place." I stop and stare at her, dark circles under her eyes and red cheeks, with Mac permanently mounted on her hip.

"Why are you here?" She asks bluntly.

"He proposed."

"Didn't you tell him you found a place and are moving out?"

"Yes. I reminded him I was clear it was temporary when I

started staying there. He told me I should stay and I wasn't moving. That was last night before he took me out."

"Why'd you agree to go out with the jerk?"

"Trying to give the ass a chance. He's been gracious and I appreciate his sugar daddiness. He was talking like he wanted to be in a relationship with me," I mumble.

"None of that sounds like anything that would impact you. What am I missing?"

"I thought we were going to the club."

"That makes more sense."

I glare at her ready to judge her opinion of me then realize how well she understands my inner ho.

"You can't just come and go as you please. Yes, the door is always open for you, but I can't handle the drama with the no sleep," she glares at me. "How are you still standing?"

"I wasn't given a choice. Which seems to be Maddux's theme. He's all about him."

Ashe gazes around the room full of questions, "Are you going back? Why are you here? Did you answer his proposal? Where's your stuff?"

That's my bestie. "What I could grab on my quick exit is in my trunk."

"So, you declined."

"I told my sugar daddy no," I cover my face to hide my confusion and the tears that aren't obeying my command to stay in place. "Why are they so stupid?"

"It's part of male genetics, but I made one of them so I can't think like that anymore. I can't handle this right now. Mac needs to sleep so I can sleep and you need sleep." She stops on that note and stares at me, "Go to bed."

"What?"

"It's the easiest thing I can handle right now and get something crossed off my list. Eliminate a piece of drama and take care of you."

"Are you pregnant again or something?"

"Don't even say those words! Go to your room." She turns around and I want to tell her she's not my mom, but why should I argue? All I've wanted to do all day is to go to bed.

I turn and walk away from her, "Ashe... always my ride or die. Love you."

"Love you, too. Glad you're back." Less than five seconds later she's yelling for Jonah. I think it's his turn.

I open the door to my room and find a pair of noise cancelling headphones still wrapped in cellophane sitting on my bed. She did miss me and understands the problem. I unwrap them immediately and connect them to my phone. Kicking my shoes off, I find my soft jammies, change and climb into bed. Lights-out in one room of the house, I scroll my many playlists for something to relax me.

The last couple of days has me cherishing memories and running them like movies in my head. I put my mellow with oldies playlist on shuffle and close my eyes.

Visions of Ashe and I over the years roll through my memories. The crazy outfits we wore. The trouble we got into even when she tried to reel me in. She's always had my back. Living together has been the easiest thing I've ever done. I don't want to move, but it's time for both of us to get on with our lives. We would still be roommates in our 70's if it weren't for Mac and that's a good thing. You never know, we may have been those crazy women that live together and party inappropriately in our 80s. I can imagine us flashing people at Mardi Gras for beads with our old lady, saggy-ass boobs hanging down to our waist and a Sazerac in our hands with bright colored feather boas around our necks. It doesn't matter where life takes us, we will always have each other. The peanut butter to my jelly and it will never go stale.

I survey the room I've slept in for years and consider sleeping in a different bed, having different furniture—living on my own. I'm good with it, but I've never lived alone. When I hear a noise I can't assume it's Ashe and let it go. Maybe I can blame it on a neighbor? What about different noises? I'm used to the rattles of the pipes and house here. The sound of the neighbor slamming the door on his car and wrestling with the lock on his front door, or the dog in the yard behind us barking up a storm—all things that are part of my world. It was different when it was just us. The crying baby and early morning alarms don't belong in my world.

My playlist takes me back to Maddux. Why'd I pick a list with love songs? We've had our moments. Me moving doesn't impact us, or at least I don't think it does. Maybe I shouldn't have gone to him when I needed a place to crash. Not the first time I made a bad decision and it won't be the last. We all do things we shouldn't when we are sleep deprived, drunk, and blinded by love. Maddux has been the center of my bad decisions when it comes to men. Ashe wasn't kidding when she referred to my Maddux Phase. I did anything and everything for him, and to him, on his schedule. No other man existed. I gave up sleep for him. I was late to work for him. I don't understand why when I remember the things I did. I'm going with love blinders. I don't regret things. Everything is part of living and character building. But what am I supposed to do when he expects things from me based on the past? He's obviously not prepared to consider that I have a life beyond him and my world no longer revolves around him—and hasn't in over a year. Still, did I make a huge mistake telling him no? Yes, he's a sugar daddy which has its benefits. I would never have to deal with him thinking I should support him and he would never scoff at spending money. The giant diamond he proposed with says everything. The thing is, I don't need a big ring. I'd prefer something that I don't have to worry about getting my hand chopped off for. Dude just go chop off the chick's finger, it'll cover two months' rent. Or whatever it may be that someone might be addicted to or catches their fancy. He needs to accept me for who I am. I'm a club girl that enjoys comfort food and hard liquor, and I work for everything I want. Not a fancy wine connoisseur who eats bugs off the ocean floor and enjoys getting spun around ballroom dance style who's going to agree with everything because that's what he wants.

Regardless, the old school slow songs take me to Maddux's arms on the dance floor. The lyrics to the different songs each taking me to a different time.

My eyes closed, I finally get my brain to rest and sleep.

CHAPTER ELEVEN

RAYE

A knock on my bedroom door wakes me from a dead sleep, "Yea?"

"Jonah had a schedule change this morning. Can we do lunch and shopping today?" Ashe asks through the door with excitement in her voice.

"I'm in. What time?" I reply groggily enjoying my warm bed.

"11am."

"What time is it now?"

"9am."

"I'll be ready." Sleep? I gaze around my room and sit up, taking inventory of everything I have to pack. I get up and shower, anxious for the day ahead of me.

Refreshed and ready to go, I unload my trunk and leave it piled on my bed. I snag boxes and packing paper from the evidence that someone in the house has an online shopping problem and get my luggage out and open. I pack my overnight bag with my necessities and a couple days' worth of clothes. I empty the drawers of my dresser into suitcases. I box up the little things I have collected that have been living on the shelf around my room. Everything from trophies and photos to knick-knacks and souvenirs, cleaning the layers of dust bunnies off and packing it all carefully. I tie my sentimental stuffies up in a garbage bag and grab some kitchen bags for the closet. I organize my closet, dividing everything up so club clothes are in one bag, dresses are in another bag, and so forth. Might as well make it easy on myself to get moved in and organized.

"Hey! I'm ready when you are," Ashe startles me. "Wow. You made some progress this morning. And look at you, all cute and awake," she chuckles.

"Thought I should get started. You really want to keep the furniture?"

"Yes. All of it. Exactly like it is. And the bedding set."

"Are you keeping my old pillows?"

"No. Those are going in the trash and we are both getting new ones."

The tone in her voice tells me she already has a plan. "So, where are we going?"

"We're taking my car because it's bigger, just in case we need room. I've got a list of things we need to get. Let's get out of here and stop for coffee, we can go over the list there."

"Yes, ma'am," I've learned to accept that my bestie always has a plan. At first it was annoying because it was my thing, but early on it occurred to me that it's work I don't have to do so why not let her? She's inherently more organized than I am anyway and much less likely to be distracted by a squirrel... *Oh look at that shiny... Check out the ass on that guy... Was that? No! It couldn't be... Clearance Rack!*

We stop at our favorite cafe for coffee, having a seat at the counter. Ashe pulls a notebook out of her bag before the waitress can take our order, "We have a lot to get done. If we can get it all done today it would be best, so you have everything and don't have to wait on anything to get delivered. Also, I'm not going to get another whole day for at least a week and it will be so much easier to try furniture without Mac strapped to me."

The waitress stops, "Haven't seen you ladies in a while. What can I get for you? Coffees?"

"Yes, please," we say in unison.

"Would you like anything else?"

"Do you have *the pancakes*?" Ashe inquires quietly as if she's being a bad girl.

"Are you referring to the special cinnamon pecan pancakes with the cream cheese layers?"

Ashe nods.

"Would you like a short stack?"

Ashe stares at me and turns back to the waitress, "Full stack to share please and extra cream cheese."

"Coming right up."

"I don't know why I ordered that. We don't have time for that."

"We need nourishment to get through the day," I smile at her and laugh. "It's not like you ordered hot fudge sundaes for breakfast."

"Those are always so good here. Extra whipped cream. Yum."

I continue to defend her, "Besides, it gives us time to go over the battle plan for the day."

"Absolutely," she's back to her notebook, flipping through to find the page she wants. "I've got your apartment diagrammed by room with a list of what you need. I also did a bit of recon to see who's having furniture sales and who has product in stock so you don't have to order and wait." She hands me her notebook, "What do you think?"

"I think you don't need to buy me all new furniture. I can take the old stuff from the house and you can have the new furniture." When did she have time to do all of this?

"That's not what I asked, do the lists look good and complete?"

"Yes," I reply, my opinion being completely ignored.

"I can buy new furniture whenever I want it. It's not time for that. I refuse to become obsessed with searching for furniture that's easy to clean and has soft corners. We are buying adult furniture for your place today," she states emphatically.

I crinkle my nose, "Are you sure we shouldn't be looking for furniture that's easy to clean? It's my place. You aren't going to be there to pick up after me and you know I'm not good at those things."

"You are going to have to learn, but I will take it into consideration," she replies with a slight bit of exasperation.

Steaming hot coffees are set down in front of us with a variety of sweeteners and creamers. I immediately wrap my fingers around the mug to absorb its warmth and bring it to my lips for a sip. I set it back down and add vanilla and hazelnut creamer until it's a warm sandy shade. We're both silent, enjoying our caffeine hit, when the pancakes are placed on the counter with an extra dish of cream cheese and whipped butter.

"Can I get you ladies anything else? Syrup? An extra plate?"

Ashe answers before I can, "This will work perfectly. Thank you."

"Keep the coffee coming. We are going to need it today," I add and Ashe nods.

The pancakes are luscious, creamy, nutty, and fluffy all at the same time. We cut the stack into quarters with our forks and spoon the cream cheese into the crevices in the middle to have more coverage on the pancakes. We dig in and enjoy the delightful bites with sips of coffee intermingled.

We are ready to get to business as the sugar high hits us and I'm along for the ride, following Captain Ashe's lead for the day. She handles everything. There's no questions beyond, "Is it comfortable? Do you like the furniture style? Do you have any patterns or colors in mind?" It's purchased and scheduled for delivery. First the complete bedroom set and new mattress, bed frame, dresser, headboard, mirror, and nightstands. Then a small dinette set with four chairs, that folds in half to push against the wall with built in storage for two of the chairs. Next the living room which starts with a gorgeous shaggy rug in alternating waves of blue and tan to orange shades that remind me of the sun setting over the ocean. It's huge and I wonder if it will fit, but Ashe says it will be fine. A velvety sofa and matching round chair and a half that are almost the same color as my coffee. A bean shaped glass coffee table and matching end table. A thin armoire that will fit over my TV mounted on the wall and hides my electronics. It just keeps going. Artwork for every room in the house. All the accessories anyone could want for the bathrooms, from rugs to the shower curtain with matching towels, and fancy little organizers for the vanity.

"I don't need that many towels. It's only me. Three or Four sets is more than enough and that green doesn't match the burgundy," I provide feedback.

Ashe smiles, "The avocado green is for me. I think it's time for a refresh." She tosses everything else in the basket for her bathroom.

"What's left on the list?"

"Kitchen is next, then bedding," she says.

"When is break time? Afternoon snack? Happy hour maybe?"

"We should do both!"

We walk through kitchen gadgets and appliances. Ashe is enthralled with the new coffee makers and tools. We keep walking without any purchase and end up at the food court. We each get a slice and sit down to relax, giving our feet a break. It has been a mission. I watch Ashe get herself organized, "You know you really didn't have to do this. Thank you for everything."

"I want to. I want your stuff to stay right where it is so it's like you're still there. It's part of our evolution and it's my fault. You didn't plan for this," her lips turn to a frown.

"It was going to happen sooner or later. We both need to have a life on our own. I'm not going anywhere. Well, down the street and up a few floors," I chuckle. "Why don't I take the old coffee maker and kitchen stuff? You buy new stuff for the house?"

She glares at me, "I like the kitchen tools. They're all broken in. Maybe the coffee maker."

"I don't need that much stuff, maybe I just take a couple pieces and be good?"

"I'm not breaking up the sets. Everyone should have service for eight."

"I only need ice cream bowls, a big bowl for popcorn, and a couple mugs for coffee and those microwavable individual cake mix things," I'm no chef. "Honestly, I can eat the popcorn straight from the microwave bag."

Ashe rolls her eyes at me, "And silverware because you can't stir your coffee or mix the individual cake mix without it."

I shrug, "I've used my finger before."

"Well, you need a spoon for ice cream then," she argues.

"Actually..." I start and she cuts me off.

"Don't say it. You can't eat ice cream with your finger."

"No, that doesn't work well. But, if you let it melt a little or microwave it for a few seconds you can drink it. Still tastes good. Oh, I need cups." I'm not worried about what we get or don't get. I can fill in the missing pieces. I'm not sure what has been purchased and what hasn't.

Ashe checks her phone and grimaces.

"Everything okay?"

"I missed texts from Jonah. My sound was off," Ashe is quiet for a minute.

"And?"

"Everything is fine. He wasn't sure what time to feed Mac and how long he usually takes his nap."

"Sounds like a good learning experience for him."

"Yes, as long as he changes his diaper and remembers to burp him. He hasn't had much time alone with Mac. I'm always there."

"A great reason to have scheduled dates with me."

"Mighty Midge said the same thing," Ashe chuckled under her breath. "Apparently, Jonah needs more training."

We finish up shopping and both end up with a new toaster, a new coffee maker, and new bedding sets. The thrift store is going to be getting a donation.

CHAPTER TWELVE

TRUCK

Truck: What time are we meeting for our monthly busi-
ness meeting today?
Vincent: I can't today.
Truck: Is there something I should know about?
Vincent: I'm busy.
Truck: Too busy for your boss?
Vincent: My busy is for you.
Truck: What am I having you do now?
Vincent: Help out the new tenant.
Truck: I knew she was going to be trouble.
Vincent: She has no idea what I'm doing.
Vincent: I had no idea what I was agreeing to, but I'm
making the best of it.
Truck: What are you doing for her that she isn't
aware of?
Vincent: You're interrupting my flow.
Vincent: Can we talk about this later.

Truck: I'd like to know what I'm paying you to do right now.

Vincent: Meeting delivery men and supervising delivery and set up.

Truck: That shouldn't take long.

Vincent: All day long. Moving service is delivering boxes, furniture and everything else is getting delivered from...

Truck: ?

Vincent: Hold on. I have to count.

Vincent: Seven different places.

Vincent: It didn't sound bad when she said all the deliveries would be arriving the same day. Why would I think all day? Seven different deliveries?

Truck: I thought you said the new tenant isn't involved.

Vincent: Her bestie was by and wanted to see the apartment before they went furniture shopping.

Vincent: Seemed harmless until I got the floor plan showing where everything was to be placed and the delivery schedule.

Truck: So, are they delivering right now?

Vincent: No.

Truck: I can meet you there for our meeting.

Vincent: I'm busy.

Truck: What are you doing?

Vincent: If you must know I decided to make the best of it and I'm trying a mosaic tile project out on the kitchen backsplash.

Truck: Not paint this time?

Vincent: I'm versatile. It's going to look like a sunrise with pieces of colored glass mixed with a ceramic background.

This is stupid. He's in the unit next door to mine. I drop my phone and walk next door, "I see. I'm sure it will be unique and another valuable artistic addition to the building."

Vin turns quickly, "Why'd you make me text that long if you were just coming in anyway?"

"How much is this piece of art costing me?" I sigh as I watch my profits for the month decrease.

"Most of it is salvaged," Vin states.

"I like the idea of recycling. Sometimes that ends up costing more than purchasing new, but I prefer to reuse," I nod waiting for the ball to drop.

Vin smiles with a sense of being let off the hook.

"How much is the rest of it?" I ask clearly.

"Not much," Vin hem-haws.

"In numbers please."

"Under $200 in tools and everything," he says quickly.

"And how about the hours I'm paying you to work on it?"

"That doesn't count. I'm stuck here waiting on deliveries anyway. Might as well be upgrading the unit."

"Uh huh. Have you considered that the tenant might not like your 'upgrade'?" I gesture at him with finger quotes.

"It's not a problem. The tenant hasn't seen the unit."

"Everyone doesn't have the same appreciation for art that you do, Vin," I say in a polite tone not wanting to offend him. He side-eyes me, "I mean Vincent. And, if they like art, it doesn't mean they like your art. I'm sorry if that's hard to hear, it's just that people have different tastes."

"I know that. If they don't like me they probably shouldn't live here," the latter part mumbled under his breath.

I pinch the bridge of my nose and close my eyes, "Permanent or semi-permanent or built in art is not always a good thing."

Vin turns to glare at me and his mouth drops theatrically, "How dare you!"

"Consider us…"

Vin cuts me off, "I have many, many times." He nibbles on his lower lip and raises his eyebrows.

"Not like that. For instance, we like different types of music yet we get along fine."

"I'm a smart man. You don't have to talk to me like you're going to upset me. Do you pay attention to the work I do here? Everything I do here is mainstream in color and pattern. I'm an artiste."

"What about the mural of nudes on the wall in unit 101?" I chuckle.

"That's my apartment. It doesn't count."

"This apartment…" I stop myself before the words "looks like an easter egg" fly out of my mouth, "Is colorful."

"Yes, it goes well with the sunlight it gets. All complementary and clean with the stark white crown molding and trim throughout the apartment."

"I'd never have considered blue, green, pink, and orange rooms all in the same apartment, but you are the artist," I comment not able to get over the resemblance to a basket of easter eggs.

Vin glares at me, "You have no appreciation of color. That's cobalt teal in the living room, muted cadmium green in the kitchen, gold ochre in the bedroom, and the bathroom is a custom mix I had made because every shade of pink looked like bubble gum."

"That makes a lot more sense," I button my lip not wanting to get into it any further and expecting to have a tenant request to paint. "What's the tape on the floor?"

"That's for the delivery men. She left me a roll of tape to mark out where everything goes, so it's easier when things arrive," he glares at me. "The bestie is nothing like the tenant. Night and day. They must balance each other."

"Why'd you agree to receive the deliveries in the first place?"

"It just happened. It's like she's got Jedi powers or something," he waves me off.

"Why that color in the bedroom? It doesn't seem relaxing," I ask and wish I hadn't.

"Perfect background for the mural I have planned."

"Does the tenant know her apartment is your canvas?"

"I told you it won't be an issue. Will you just trust me for once?" Vin shakes his head. "I've had enough today. Let me work on this and forget I was conned into being a lackey."

CHAPTER THIRTEEN

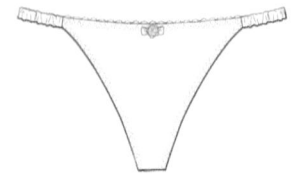

RAYE

A couple of days later, I unlock the door to my new apartment and walk in for the first time with my bestie right behind me. I had no clue what to expect. My surprise was two-fold. All of the furniture is in place with suitcases, boxes and small deliveries lined up neatly along the wall in the bedroom. Which brings me to the second thing, the walls. It's like a box of crayons threw up on the walls throughout my apartment. I turn to Ashe, "Do the walls in here make you feel like you are in an easter basket?"

She glares back at me, "The windows let in good light, the building is well-kept, and the paint is fresh. Maybe the maintenance man is color blind? I was hoping the furniture and things we chose would help mellow it out a bit."

What? "You've already been in my apartment."

"Well, yeah. I needed to have more details before we went shopping and the property manager guy is fab! He supervised the deliveries."

"So, you were in my apartment before me and already made friends with my property manager?"

"Of course. You think I'm going to let you move to a place I haven't checked out?"

"I am an adult and able to make decisions," I remind her.

Ashe gets in front of me, face to face, "You didn't look at the apartment or take a tour of the building before signing the lease agreement, did you?"

"I went with my gut."

"How's the easter egg basket agreeing with your gut? Feeling widgey?"

"If you had looked for an apartment as much as I had, you'd have jumped on this one when it became available too."

"Actually, I would've given in to my bestie and rented the place with the beach view and lower rent because it has the best property manager ever," she grins like she just dropped the mic.

A knock on the door we left open behind us has us both jumping out of our skins. We turn to find possibly the most gorgeous man I've ever seen standing in my doorway. "Hello ladies. I heard some noise next door so I thought I'd check it out. Don't let me get in the middle of your argument. I'm the neighbor, my name's Truck," he extends his hand to shake.

I take his hand immediately but no words come out because I'm too busy checking him out in his jeans and snug fitting t-shirt.

Ashe has my back, "I'm Ashley and this is Raye. She's my bestie and your new neighbor. Not an argument, just a discussion." Ashe grabs my arm and smirks at me, "Never mind, I understand why you rented it now. I'm going to run down to the car and grab the care package I put together for you. You'll be fine here tonight. Be right back." She leaves shaking her head.

I need to get my brain working over my libido. "Nice to

meet you. Truck? That's an interesting name. Where does that come from?"

He grins in a kind of one-sided way, "I know how to handle the off-road curves."

"I bet you do," I say out loud without thinking.

"Anyway, it's nice to meet you, Raye. I'm sure I'll be seeing you around," he nods. "Have a good evening." He nods and I swear he winks at me as he leaves my doorway.

Did it just get twenty degrees hotter in here? I'm pulling at the front of my shirt to let some air in when Ashe gets back.

"Hot and bothered in thirty seconds or less?" She giggles.

I shut the door behind her quickly. "He can obviously hear everything when the door is open."

"Did you see the way the jeans fit that man? And, you know he's tan like that all over."

Ashe gazes at me wide-eyed, "Just remember he's your neighbor. You will have to see him the next day and he will see every guy you bring home, just like you will see all the women he brings home." She giggles, "He will be nice to look at every time."

"A wise woman once told me that women have needs. I might have needs," I gaze at her innocently.

"You've spent most of the last few weeks with Maddux. I'm sure you've been satisfied recently."

"I guess I need to get the place ready so I can get settled tonight," I say, unsure of myself.

"Don't worry. I'm going to put away the things I brought in the care package for you and then I'll help you get the bed made and a few other things before I go home. You'll be fine," Ashe says assuring me.

"What's in the care package?"

"Ice cream, popcorn, water, 2% milk, cereal, coffee, toaster waffles, peanut butter, a loaf of bread, grape jelly, a box of those individual mug cake mixes, string cheese, candy bars, salsa, and tortilla chips."

"I'll never have to leave home," I say thinking that's everything I need for days.

"I'm just putting away the things that need to be refrigerated. The rest I will leave on the counter for you to figure out how you want to organize your kitchen."

We walk into my bedroom, "Who paints a bedroom orange?"

"I don't know, but I don't think that mural of a sunset was there when I was here before. It's new," Ashe stops and walks away. Then returns, "The mosaic backsplash in the kitchen is new, too."

"What am I missing here? Did I move into an artist's gallery?"

Ashe cocks here head to the side and back, "At least the artist has some skill. The colors in each room go well together, just not the best for different rooms in the same apartment. The orange is only on two walls and part of it is covered. We could get more artwork."

"You mean a wall-sized tapestry?" I chuckle, "I do like the mural. It's somehow relaxing even with all the orange."

We put the soft misty grey sheets on my bed layered with a new steel grey plush blanket and a king-sized quilt to cover my queen-sized bed. The neutral blues and greys in the small floral print of the quilt somehow complement the orange of the room. We stuff new fluffy pillows into the pillow cases and shams, and toss the multitude of throw pillows in different shapes, sizes and textures onto my bed. The burnt orange, yellow, and blue pillows she talked me into make sense now amongst the varying shades of grey.

We put the shower curtain up easily with four hands and the tension rod. The curtain with pink, burgundy, and white triangles overlapping looks like organic leaves even though they are all straight lines, and bring the pink of the walls together with the burgundy towels and accents.

Ashe gazes at me with tears filling her eyes, "Okay. One more thing I need to make sure is ready for you before I leave you here." A tear slips down her cheek and she turns quickly toward the kitchen, "We need to set up your coffee maker, run water through it and then give it a test run."

"Ashe, I can do it. I will be fine. Your place will always be home and you are always welcome here. It's okay, you can go home. I know Mac needs you and you need rest," I say in the sincerest voice I have.

"Do you want me to leave? You've got that guy coming over and he's just waiting for me to go?"

"No. It's just me tonight. I need to do this and you have done more than anyone could ask for."

"A housewarming party!" Ashe exclaims out of nowhere.

"What? Why?"

"It's your first place. You need a housewarming party. We can invite friends and your neighbors to meet people."

"That's not necessary. Let's not and say we did."

"That proves it. You'll never meet your neighbors if you don't have a housewarming."

"Let me get unpacked and organized and then we can talk about it."

"I'll call your property manager tomorrow. I'm sure he has a way of inviting everybody. Let's plan on next Friday evening."

"Really, I don't want to have a party."

"It will be fun. I'll bring Jonah and Mac. So there will be at least four of us," she stops and looks around. "Okay, I'm getting out of here. I will talk to you tomorrow and see you early on Friday to make sure you are ready for the party, if not sooner." She wraps her arms around me, "Always my ride or die, love you Raye," she turns and leaves quickly. I'm sure trying to hide the tears rolling down her face just like the ones on mine. It's time. We all need to be grownups at some point.

CHAPTER FOURTEEN

TRUCK

*Y*ou did your quick meet and greet, so you're a good neighbor and have seen what she looks like. There's nothing wrong with that. Just being a good neighbor.

The problem is her curves have me wanting to explore them and I can't do that. I don't have anything to do with women in my building. Her angelic face with her contrary mouth, with those curls falling around it that somehow seem to move with her hips. I bet she plays music and dances around her apartment in her panties when she's home alone. Her eyes remind me of gazing down into the ocean when I'm out on my surfboard and they simply sparkle with the strawberry blond.

Truck: You did this on purpose.

Vincent: I'm sorry, is this work? I'm off duty.

Truck: This is most definitely not work.

Vincent: In that case, would you like to come over?

Vincent: We can talk over Project Runway and wine.

He always does this to me. I find myself pinching the bridge of my nose again and pounding my forehead against the wall.

Truck: Wine isn't my thing. Some of the chicks on Project Runway are hot, still not my thing.

Vincent: So sad. It's fabulous this season.

Truck: Don't distract me.

Vincent: You have no idea what it means to me when you are distracted by me.

Vincent: There's a reason I don't give up.

I'm just going to come straight out with it or I'll never get it out.

Truck: Did you rent to her on purpose?

Vincent: I didn't rent the unit on accident, if that's what you mean.

Truck: You know what I mean.

Vincent: Sorry, I don't.

Truck: You rented to her with intentions of setting us up.

Vincent: I thought I've been clear that I'm saving you for me.

Now he's just fucking with me.

Truck: You rented the apartment next to mine to a beautiful single woman who is my type and appears to be my age.

Vincent: I did?

Truck: Yes, you did.

Vincent: What a cowinkidink.

Truck: Cowinkidink my ass!

Vincent: Is there another definition for cowinkidink that I'm not aware of. I've never heard it used as a verb before.

Truck: Tell me why.

Vincent: Do you expect me to start quoting Backstreet Boys lyrics?

Truck: You know I can't have anything to do with women in the building.

Vincent: Why is that?

Vincent: Heartache?

Vincent: A Mistake?

Truck: We've been through this before.

Truck: It's a disaster. It can go wrong in so many ways.

Truck: I don't want to move again.

Vincent: It doesn't have to go wrong.

Vincent: It could be right.

Vincent: Ok… gotta go now. Goodnight!

He may not have done it intentionally, but he's definitely appreciating the situation. I wouldn't be surprised if he didn't expect it.

Music starts playing in the unit next door, followed by a little squeal and clapping. Yep, dancing around in her panties.

THE NEXT MORNING...

Vincent: The whole building has been invited to a
housewarming party at the new tenant's place.
Vincent: Friday evening and you are expected to be
there.
Vincent: I suggest you wear the old-school jeans, they
accent your package the best.
Vincent: Be sure you take a shower sometime before
then. Nobody likes a stinky neighbor.
Vincent: The bestie left me a voicemail overnight
asking to announce it to the building.
Vincent: Apparently she can't wait to meet me and I'm
an angel for helping out with the deliveries.
Vincent: Since you haven't responded I'm going to
assume you are still sleeping.
Vincent: I hope you are dreaming of me <3

Another appearance and chance to screw everything up.
Just what I need.

CHAPTER FIFTEEN

RAYE

I've spent the last few days getting things put away or hung on the wall. I've got the kitchen organized with all the stuff Ashe said I needed to have and will probably never use. I purchased a few things that we missed and have more than I need.

Lamps. Seriously, how did we forget lamps? I bought a cool wicker chandelier for the living room, which led to me finding Vincent to borrow a ladder and Vincent climbing the ladder because apparently tenants can borrow the ladder but are not allowed to use it. I bought a lamp for my nightstand and then went back to buy another because I have two nightstands even if I only use one and it made my whole bedroom off balance, which is what Ashe said would happen if I only had one nightstand (along with some crazy mumbo jumbo about how I might wish I had the second nightstand at some point and then I wouldn't be able to get it, though when I told her I don't have enough dildos for two nightstands she covered her ears and said "I was thinking a living one not a blow up one.") I also bought a floor lamp for the living room with a dimming feature, in case I want to set the mood.

And, while I was out I decided to try being an adult—I bought a plant. The green kind, with the long vines and leaves that seem to grow no matter what, seemed like the right choice for a beginner like me. It adds some life to my breakfast bar, goes with the green walls, and gets plenty of light. Plus, it gives me the best chance at succeeding at keeping something alive besides myself. It's in a plastic pot and set inside a ceramic goldfish, so it brings some more orange to the open kitchen and living room area and maybe ties the whole apartment together better. Though, now I'm a bit frightened by the thought of a huge goldfish. I even had a dream that I was swimming in the ocean and I was attacked by a school of goldfish. There was a woman swimming near me that keep calling out for "Pluckie," it was the strangest thing.

When I finally had a chance to sit and relax on my couch, I draped the new navy-blue chenille throw blanket I bought over my legs and propped up the additional throw pillows I bought while I was at the store. I couldn't resist the pillows, they're the same colors as the rug and one has a sunset on it. I lean back and snuggle in with my phone in hand...

Raye: What should I get to be ready for the house-warming party?

Ashley: Nothing.

Raye: I need to have snacks for my neighbors.

Ashley: I already ordered everything to be delivered.

Raye: What about paper plates or cups?

Ashley: It's handled.

Raye: What are we having?

Ashley: I ordered a crudités and hummus platter.

Ashley: I've got everything to mix up some sangria in the pitcher we bought that you said you'd never use.

Ashley: I suppose you could get a bag of chips and microwave a bag of popcorn.

Ashley: I didn't get any beer.

Raye: That's it?

Ashley: Get your music set up and have something playing in the background.

Raye: I did that the first night I was here.

Ashley: Empty the ice maker into a bowl in the freezer and make more ice. We'll need it.

Ashley: I'll be there early to help get everything ready.

Raye: We don't have to have a housewarming.

Ashley: Yes you do.

My doorbell rings and I find a package with my name on it. I cut open the box to find matching plates, cups, napkins, and plasticware.

I turn on some music and make a practice batch of popcorn with the new-to-me microwave. I don't want my apartment smelling like burnt popcorn when my new neighbors meet me.

I GET HOME from work on Friday and find Ashe parked in front of my building waiting for me.

"I was about to go find your property manager and get him to let me in," Ashe says impatiently.

"Hi! It's nice to see you, too!" I say to her with fake cheer.

She rolls her eyes, "We have to get ready."

"Where's Jonah and Mac?"

"Jonah is bringing Mac with him later, so we have time to get ready first."

"Okay, what can I help unload?" I ask.

"Let's start with these," she says as she pops open the hatch on her SUV and wrangles a half dozen balloons in the ocean breeze.

I glare at her, "Balloons?"

"People need to know where the party is."

I grab the additional box of stuff she brought with her and we take the elevator up to my apartment.

I open the door and she examines my space, "You've gotten a lot done and you've been shopping." She stops and stares at me, "We forgot lamps! I love this wicker chandelier. It looks great in here with everything put away and the extra touches you've added."

"Thank you," I smile appreciating the kudos. "What do we need to get ready?"

"We need to make the sangria first, so it has some time to meld. Find a way to anchor the balloons by your door. Get the platter open and moved to a dish, so we can throw away the store-bought evidence before anyone gets here. You already have your bowls out and the paper goods opened, so we are ahead of the game."

I turn the music on and shake my hips a bit as I walk through my apartment. I'm going to say that again. My apartment. I slice up oranges and limes while Ashe gets the red wine open and we toss it all together in the pitcher with some lemon lime soda. Then she pulls a fifth of rum out of a bag and adds that, as well as part of a frozen fruit juice concentrate. I like where this is going. She stirs it and places it in the refrigerator.

"Don't we get to try it?" I ask with a grin on my face.

"Not yet, and you need to be ready to meet new people."

"Even more reason to get a head start, don't you think?"

Ashe side-eyes me and we keep going to get ready.

When everything is ready it reminds me of an adult's apartment. Who lives here? It can't be me.

There's a knock on the door and I open it to find Vincent, "Welcome!" I reach up and give him a quick one-armed hug around the neck. "Come on in." I point to Ashe, "This is Ashley, my sister from another mister."

He smiles and surveys my space oddly, "Nice to finally meet you after chatting on the phone." He turns to me, "This woman is in charge."

"She always has been," I reply and spy Ashe taking the sangria out of the refrigerator. "I learned to accept it and appreciate it a long time ago."

"You're here and know the building best, must be the best person to enlist for help. It's nice to put a face to your voice," Ashe chimes in.

"I love that you played up to my sunset and sunrise design in here," Vincent comments.

Ashe and I glare at each other immediately.

"Do you do all the painting?" I ask.

"Yes, the painting, the tile on the backsplash, everything artistic, and all the maintenance that doesn't get my hands dirty. This is one of my favorite units, so I hope you like the color. You've really done well decorating with it and bringing it together," he says.

It's still a bit of an easter basket to me but it's getting better, "I love the sunset mural and the mosaic in the kitchen."

"Thank you," he replies graciously.

"Please make yourself at home. I have snacks and sangria at your disposal on the breakfast bar."

Vincent hands me a small gift bag and continues to the kitchen to check out the spread.

I'm suddenly nervous that he's the only person who will show up and find myself fidgeting with the music. Maybe something a little more upbeat would be good, I switch to my club mix.

My doorbell rings and I answer it to find Truck wearing old jeans that have been fitted to him over time and accentuate his assets. All of his assets. Perfectly taut across his butt, yet still showing off what he has to offer in the front, and loose enough at the waist to make me wonder about the sexy happy trail that's peeking out. His faded Mr. Zog's Sex Wax t-shirt has seen better days with pin holes and a hem that's ripped, highlighting the muscles in his shoulders and too short to reach his low-slung jeans. Unbelievably sexy in his own thrown together without a care and no time to comb my hair sort of way. He runs his fingers through his hair on command, as if my thought was a reminder to comb it.

I invite him in as he runs his thumb across his lower lip, "Hi Truck, come on in and make yourself at home. It's nice to see you again. I think you know everyone that's here so far."

He nods, "You've done a lot in a short time. This place doesn't look like a carton of easter eggs anymore." He stops and starts, "Please take that as a compliment."

"I will," I giggle and inhale his citrus mixed with a beach bonfire scent as he steps in and moves toward my kitchen.

Ashe joins the conversation as he approaches her, "Truck, right?"

He nods.

"Where does your name come from?" Ashe asks.

Truck quirks his head, "I arrived earlier than expected. We

were on a family road trip and Mom had to pull off the freeway in Truckee to deliver me."

"That's one way to get a name," Ashe comments and I stay quiet.

Truck shrugs, "Parents. At least they didn't name me something boring like Vincent."

Vincent glares at him and comments in an affectionate tone, "Asshole."

The doorbell rings again as the conversation continues in the kitchen and I wish I had a tall glass of sangria in my hand. I open the door to an older woman with grey wavy hair and a plate covered in foil, "Hi, I'm Raye and I'm the new tenant." I extend my hand to shake, but she can't because her hands are full.

She smiles and hands me the plate, "I'm Agnes. I live at the end of the hall. It's nice to meet you. Nobody follows etiquette anymore. It's refreshing from a young person like yourself."

"Thank you," chalk that one up for Ashe. "Thank you for joining us. Please come in. This plate feels warm."

"It is. Fresh baked chocolate chip cookies," she smiles.

I unwrap the plate as I lead her to the kitchen, "This is my best friend Ashley, and I'm sure you know Vincent and Truck."

"Truck? No honey, his name's Tuck," she says confidently standing next to him. "He's a very helpful young man and never causes a ruckus."

"Actually, my name is Truck," he corrects her and gives her a consolation side hug.

Agnes glares at him, "Truck? Who names their baby Truck?"

Truck smiles kind of one-sided, "My mom, she always wanted a truck."

Agnes pours a glass of sangria and walks off mumbling

under her breath, "I never. Who does that! And he's such a good boy…"

Truck and Vincent make eye contact and go for the cookies, obviously not the first time they've had them. I grab one to try before they are gone and I'm glad I made a friend with my etiquette—the cookies are gooey and delicious. I wonder if Vincent asked her about those before he rented to her?

I try the hummus with some pita and get a bottle of water since Ashe gave me the mom look when I reached for the sangria. I get it, save it for the guests.

There's something about the apartment with people, it does have a more homey vibe. I hear the door again and go to answer.

Ashe squeezes by me as I open the door, "I'll be right back."

There's a thin woman with long straight dark hair at my door, "Hi, I'm Raye. Thanks for coming."

She grabs my hand with both of hers and shakes it repeatedly, "I'm Cathy. I'm so happy to meet you. I live next door. I can't wait to get to know you. It can be so quiet around here. Nobody to talk to. I know we will be great friends."

I nod, "I'm sure we will. Come on in, my guess is you know everyone who's here."

"Yes, of course. The regulars including the punisher."

Vincent perks up, "Don't be spreading rumors, Cathy. I can hear you from over here."

"Yes sir!" She replies instantly, "Are those Agnes' cookies?"

"Yes, and they're still warm," Truck replies.

Cathy elbows her way in and takes a few before settling on my couch and playing with the fringe on my new blanket.

My doorbell rings and I abandon the glass of sangria I'm trying to sneak before Ashe gets back. I open the door to an older couple, "Welcome! I'm Raye. Thanks for coming to my housewarming."

"Hello sweetie, I'm Mary and this is my asshole Harry, I mean husband," she chuckles in her low female tone.

"It's nice to meet you both. Where do you live in the building?" I ask inquisitively.

Mary opens her mouth to speak and Harry raises his hand to shush her taking control of the conversation, "End unit on the second floor. Do you have beer?"

"Sorry, no. I have a pitcher of sangria in the kitchen and some snacks you are welcome to," I reply politely.

"You should have beer," he says grumpily.

"Stop being a dick, dear," Mary tells him loud enough for everyone to hear.

"Didn't I tell you we didn't need to bring a gift? Why would you bring a gift to someone that doesn't have beer for her guests?"

"Shut up, dear," Mary continues as they walk in and mingle with everyone.

I'm about to close the door when a handsome young man walks up, "Hello, are you Raye?"

"Yes, are you one of my new neighbors?"

"I am and thank you so much for inviting me to your home. I'm Joseph," he reaches out and shakes my hand. "I live in 310. I'm always excited to see another unit and discover what the amazing Vincent has done this time. He's got an incomparable artistic eye," he says almost fawning.

I run with it, "My unit has a sunrise and sunset theme to accent the natural light."

"Oh my gosh! That sounds fabulous," he gazes around my apartment. "And the artist himself is here! It's like attending his gallery show." He turns to me, "Do I look okay?"

I smile, "The best dressed here. Please feel free to take the self-guided tour and make yourself at home."

He gazes at me happily, "I love you! So hospitable!"

Ashe has been gone for over ten minutes and I'm starting to wonder what's going on, when she comes back through the door with Mac on her hip and Jonah at her side. I go around the room introducing everyone and Ashe bounces a happy Mac along with me so he gets to meet everyone, she's such a proud mommy.

Jonah joins the men in the kitchen, grabbing a cookie and attempting small talk, "Vin and Truck?"

"Vincent, not Vin. Please tell me you're not an asshole like him," he says gesturing to Truck.

"Only 5% asshole, 30% if you add alcohol," Jonah jokes. "Truck is unique. Is that a nickname? Where does it come from?"

"It's the name on my birth certificate. I was born in a truck," he said with that same one-sided smile.

With the party going in full swing, Ashe grabs my hand, "Are you ready for your housewarming gift?"

"You've done too much already," I reply.

She walks to the door, opens it and quickly grabs a box from the hallway. She hands it to me, "This is Birdie."

I'm wondering what the heck Ashe did when I discover the contents of the box are alive and moving around. I put the box down quickly on the floor and before I can say or do anything the top of the box moves. I take a step back.

"Don't worry. I brought you everything you need including a proper carrier. I'm just worried about you. We aren't living together anymore and I don't want you to be alone. I can't be your wing girl in the next room. When I heard her name is Birdie, well perfect wing girl!" Ashe opens the top of the box and there sits a grey striped cat with yellow green eyes and a dark pink nose, permanently sparkling for the club with white eyeliner. She jumps out of the box with finesse and wanders my apartment from corner to corner and room to room, introducing herself to everyone in attendance with her tail in the air.

I turn and whisper in Ashe's ear, "I bought a plant as a challenger to myself to keep something alive. You brought me a cat! I don't know anything about cats."

"That's why you got a cat. She's independent and will tell you if she needs anything. Jonah's going to get the cat's belongings from the hallway and put them in your bedroom. We should probably get the litter box set up, so she doesn't decide she has nowhere to do her business."

Ashe turns away to work on getting the cat settled, leaving me standing there dumbfounded. A cat. I watch as the boxes of stuff get brought in and left in my bedroom. I just finished unpacking boxes. What happened to cat box, food, and water? This cat has more belongings than I do. Huh. She did this on purpose while everyone is here so I can't go off or get mad and they all know I have a cat now. Who names a cat Birdie? Distracted by the whole thing I lose track of the cat and find her weaving around Truck's legs while he scratches her chin. Ho. Hmm. Maybe we will be friends.

Jonah drags in a six-foot tall cat tree and fits it into the corner of my bedroom. Ashe sets the cat box up in my bathroom—just when I thought I had a bathroom to myself. Then I find her in the kitchen putting food in a little ceramic dish painted with paws and setting up a fountain for the cat to drink from. There's a cat bed under the end table with balls and fake mice in it. Canisters now sit on my kitchen counter labeled Birdie's Food and Birdie's Treats. A cat hammock has been suction cupped to my bedroom window and I have a box of cat steps that are to be mounted on the wall for the beast to walk on. I thought this was my apartment and now I'm beginning to wonder who's in charge.

Ashe stands in front of me, "At least introduce yourself and try to make friends. Give her a chance. She's housebroken which is more than I can say about you."

I turn around and find Birdie jumping onto my bed and walking in circles until she lays down in a ball. That's kind of cute. I sit down on the edge of my bed to have a conversation with her and Vincent sticks his head in my room with a soft knock on my bedroom door, "You are pre-approved to have the cat. Ashley already took care of that with me and paid the pet fee." He starts to walk away and comes back, "It might be nice to have a furry roommate." He glances across the room at the cat steps, "If you'd like, I can install those for you and paint a mural around them on the wall."

Seems useless to argue with him, "That would be great. Thank you."

He nods and leaves me with Birdie. I lay back on my bed next to her and caress her tail, "I'm Raye. We're going to be roommates. Be glad Ashe didn't take you home with her and the screaming baby. I have no idea how to take care of a cat, but you're my new wing girl and I'm going to be a crazy cat lady—I'm already talking to the cat. I have to mingle with the new neighbors which you understand and have already made your rounds. I'll be back when they are all gone. Your food and water are in the kitchen and your poo box is in the bathroom. Find me if you need anything." I walk out to the living room, but in my head all I can think is "Yep, crazy cat lady."

BIRDIE

It's been a long and stressful day. I spent over an hour in a cardboard box and that's simply undignified. I was happy to be plucked from the foster home, but I didn't foresee an easy transition with the woman who picked me up. She seemed a bit high maintenance to me and I'm not looking to be a servant, I'm in search of one. This Raye person should do quite well.

She has no training, so I can mold her to my liking. All I want to do is relax and take a cat nap. Why are all of these people in my new home? Maybe this was my court here to greet me? This bed is nice and the texture of the quilt is luxurious under my paws. Yes, just a short nap…

"Isn't that a pretty kitty?" Mary asks Harry.

Who is waking me with unnecessary chatter? I open one eye slightly to ensure they are a safe distance from me. The couple. Of course, they have the scent of the superior feline clan. It makes sense that they would want to pay respect to their leader.

"It's just a cat," he replies and I watch him closely as he moves about the room. He opens a drawer and pulls out something shiny, "It's been a long time since I've seen you in a pair of these. Hubba hubba, maybe I should grab them and take them home with us for some fun?" The dirty man raises his eyebrows and smacks the woman on the ass.

Just a cat! He will be exiled! Banish him immediately and disinfect those panties.

"What are you thinking, Harry?"

"I'm more about action than words," he replies.

"Did you forget what happened the last time you had any *action*?" She asks. "Those won't fit me."

"So I ended up in the emergency room, you were satisfied weren't you?"

"Yea, but I'm not sure it was worth the three weeks of being your maid while you were stuck in bed."

"Ingrateful."

I must agree with him on that one, but I don't need anybody anyway. I lick myself. Now please, remove these people from my presence. I must sleep.

Zzz…

Wait! Who's touching me? I didn't give anyone permission to touch me. I force my eyes open to find the chin scratcher sitting next to me, disturbing my sleep and yet not paying any attention to me. Who does he think he is? This is an outrage! He smells inviting.

I observe as he stands and walks over to gaze at the glass wall. Then he turns around and sees the mess painted on the wall, probably wondering what it is like I do.

It's getting quieter and people are leaving.

Chin scratcher runs his finger across a pair of shiny panties that are hanging out of a drawer and stops, curling his finger around them and pulling them from the drawer, he holds them up and quickly shoves the small piece of material in his back pocket.

I sit up formally judging him for his actions. Chin scratching panty freak. Not proper at all. I adjust my paws on the soft material as he turns and looks at me, running his fingers through his hair and pulling the panties out of his pocket and then shoving them back in. He leaves quickly, I hear him saying goodbyes. Thief. Panty Thief. At least he could've offered to rub me some more so I could turn him down. I must remember to keep an eye on him... zzz.

CHAPTER SIXTEEN

RAYE

*T*he housewarming party went well. The cat and I shared the bed last night with no issue, she even slept close to my feet which was warm and unexpected. Though she did get up in the middle of the night to use the box and scratch at it for what must've been an hour. I asked her where she was trying to dig to, but she ignored me. When I woke up for the day and wanted to stay in my warm cozy bed she crawled up closer to me and kneaded the bed next to me with a rumbling purr until she curled back up in agreement with me to go back to sleep.

Until my phone rang. I reached for it to answer and Birdie covered her face trying to make it go away, "Hello?"

"Good morning, how's today for working on the cat steps and mural?" Vincent asks cheerfully.

"That's fine, but I'm not up and I haven't had my coffee yet," I reply on a yawn.

"Girl, I don't leave my apartment until noon on weekends. I have personal maintenance necessary to keep me looking like I'm in my thirties," he laughs. "Like sleep to keep the bags and wrinkles away."

"Perfect, come on up whenever you're ready," I chuckle and anticipate an entertaining visit with my new friend.

I should've let Ashe spend the extra money on the smart espresso and cappuccino maker. It could be brewing fresh ground coffee beans to order for me while I enjoy the warmth of my bed. I imagine the aroma waking me and pulling me from my sheets to the kitchen, floating weightlessly in anticipation of the elixir I crave. Birdie has the right idea, snuggled in the nest of blankets she's created overnight with her eyes shut tight. I get up and make my way to the kitchen, barefoot on the cold floor to start my coffee manually. I need to set the thermostat or find my slippers, and I need a throw rug in my kitchen. I grab my mug from my coffee maker as soon as its done brewing, surprised to find Birdie sitting stoically on the kitchen counter next to the coffee maker. Ashe would have a coronary, I'm wondering if the feline wants coffee. I lean against my kitchen counter with mug in hand and sip. My roommate paws at my arm and stares at me. "I don't speak cat, so you better speak English." I shake my head and watch as she jumps down and sits in front of her food bowl. She sits up straight, almost formally and pulls her feet together, then stares up at me. We may be able to communicate easier than I thought. I may have a larger learning curve than she does. I refill her food dish and she rubs against my legs before proceeding to eat. She has the right idea, I drop a waffle in the toaster and eat one of Agnes' chocolate chip cookies while I wait. I spread some peanut butter on my waffle and take it and my coffee with me to get comfy in my round chair and a half. I pull my feet up into the chair and grab the blanket from the couch to try and warm them up. As soon as I'm settled, Birdie is curled up next to my feet being my personal heater.

Agnes' cookies inspire me to research etiquette. I need to send a thank you note to the people who brought me a house-warming gift and a change of address announcement to my family and friends. Ashe will be proud that she didn't have to prod me to do it.

I'm scrolling through custom address change announce-ments and getting distracted by fancy return address labels when Vincent knocks on my door, "Good afternoon, Sir!" I say bright and cheery.

"Good afternoon to you. Don't you look relaxed and comfy in your new place," he remarks with a grin.

"I'm getting the hang of this having my own place thing. Would you like some coffee?"

"Always, please," the magic glow of caffeine addiction shining in his eyes.

"You don't have to install the steps on the wall or paint or anything. You're welcome anytime, just you with no ulterior motive," I remind him.

"I'll keep that in mind for future reference. I'm interested in what I can do with the steps. I'm envisioning a mural of a tree incorporating the steps," he stops and nibbles on his upper lip. "Also, if I install them it will be easier if I have to remove them later." He takes a breath, "That didn't come out right. Sometimes the property manager takes over. I'm sure you'll be here for years to come. I hope you are."

"I get it. You seem protective of the building. I'm happy to live in a place where people care, makes it more like home and not so much like I live alone," I say and wonder where the words come from. Birdie from a dead sleep instantly glares at me to remind me I don't live alone. I hand Vincent his coffee with a small plate of Agnes' cookies.

His eyes widen, "You do like me. I knew we would be friends." His genuine smile taking over, he sets the plate down on the coffee table and gets the box of cat steps from my bedroom.

I watch him as he happily inventories all of the pieces in the box and lays them out in a pattern on the floor. "I don't want to interrupt your artistic process, but I'm here and available to help or chat. And I'm not rushing you. I'm home all day today attempting to get used to my new digs and bonding with Birdie."

He gazes up, "Birdie?"

"Yep."

"But it's a cat and cats eat birds," he plays the part of captain obvious.

"Yes, well, Ashe wanted to make sure I had a wing woman close by and then she met Birdie."

Vincent smirks, "And now I'm making a tree for Birdie to climb."

I chuckle, "It's never-ending."

He's moving the pieces around and drawing on the wall in pencil, "I could've made a bet on who was going to show up for your housewarming party."

"How's that?"

"Cathy will take any opportunity she can to talk to anyone. She comes to my office to talk about rent every month." He perks up, "Maybe she needs a cat."

"I don't know. This feline is smart and knows how to get what she wants."

"It could be too much for her. Maybe just a mirror and she can talk to herself," he suggests.

"I don't think that's a healthy option. Maybe she needs a parrot that will repeat what she says back to her."

"Poor bird wouldn't be able to keep up with how much and

how fast she talks, no, definitely an animal without speaking capabilities," Vincent says decidedly.

"I know! She needs a goldfish. She can pretend it's talking back to her every time it opens its mouth or makes a bubble. She can name it Pluckie," I state remembering the repeating dream about being attacked by goldfish.

"Pluckie?"

"Repeating nightmare I have. I'm being attacked by a school of goldfish and a woman is calling for Pluckie. I've come to the conclusion it's the name of one of the goldfish. I hope for the woman's sake that Pluckie didn't end up in someone's mouth."

"I'm not going to ask," Vincent says.

"That's probably best. At least I'm not being attacked by something that could actually hurt me. Maybe the goldfish will eat the dead skin off like those fish that eat stuff off other fish."

"Stop. Please."

"Are you suddenly wanting to paint a pond instead of a tree?"

"What is Birdie supposed to do in a pond?" He laughs.

"Maybe Birdie could go fishing in the pond?" I laugh out loud. "Maybe Cathy should make friends with Agnes," I suggest.

"They do fine now, but there was a falling out a few years ago. Agnes baked cookies and left them at the doors of the neighbors she's friends with and Cathy swears she didn't get any. Agnes says she left them for her and believes Cathy was just lying to get more cookies. Agnes is old school proper, so she held a grudge and Cathy will never get another cookie unless she's at a housewarming or something like last night. Agnes bakes a top-notch cookie, so it's a true punishment," Vincent explains.

I quirk my head toward him, "What do you think happened in that cookie fiasco?"

"I'm pretty sure somebody took the cookies that were left at Cathy's door," he says sure of himself.

"Who would do that?" I ask, wondering who I have to watch out for and if I should just give Agnes a key to my apartment now to avoid the possibility.

Vincent shrugged and refused to make eye contact. "They're damn good cookies. You shouldn't waste calories on anything but the best."

"Case closed," I nod my head.

"In my defense, Truck dared me and provided milk to drink with the evidence."

"I get the idea you and Truck are buddies, seemed pretty thick last night," I offer my observation.

"I suppose. Really though? I hit on him and he turns me down. I contract him to do the dirty jobs around here, he refuses to do the *dirty deed* I'm interested in, rinse, wash, and repeat."

"So, what's his deal?"

"He's a charming contractor, surfer, and beach bum. He's been here forever and I doubt he ever leaves. Self-proclaimed bachelor and I've never seen him with a woman or a man for that matter. Either way, I'm not giving up," he chuckles. "Did you see the abs and ass on that man? He's like candy to me!"

"It's hard to miss the way his jeans fit perfectly and I want to know if he's tan like that all over," I say without thinking.

"I'd say that's a challenge for you to find out. He won't let me get close enough," Vincent concedes.

"I think getting it on with my neighbor might be too close for comfort and would get me in trouble. I don't want any trouble with my property manager. I've heard he's known as the punisher," I laugh.

Vincent stops what he's doing and puts down the pencil he had in his hand, "It's my job to enforce the rules and regulations of this building, including any necessary fines and punishments."

"I don't want to know what Cathy did."

"Good, it's protected by the privacy guidelines and I can't tell you," Vincent says in his business voice. "Agnes, however, can get out of anything by bribing me with cookies and she knows it. I even extended the date her rent was due and took the late fee in cookies. I gained three pounds that week and it was worth it."

I stop and focus on the line drawing on my living room wall. It starts from the floor and the tree climbs up extending over the top of the sofa to the right and fades off on the left. It's designed into my living room with the furniture in it. Puffy little clouds of leaves surround some steps, while others form branches, and some of the tree is simply paint. One of the steps is drawn to be a nest with a banner hung on it that says "Birdie." "You have an amazing ability to visualize things. I could never have imagined a tree like this with such detail and personalization."

"Does that mean you like it so far?" He asks.

"Yes I do. Very much."

"Good, help me move your rug and sofa. I don't want to accidentally get paint on anything."

I help him move the furniture and as soon as he starts painting Birdie is standing behind him following his every move with her eyes, her furry head bouncing around with his paint strokes.

I'm not sure I should go there, but, "What's the deal with Joseph?"

Vincent replies and keeps his eyes on the mural, "Can we not discuss that child?"

"No problem," the last thing I want to do is upset the punisher.

"I get that I'm an artist, but he treats me like I'm untouchable and I'm old enough to be his father. I'm totally flattered. I'm just... it makes me uncomfortable. He keeps asking me to do more to his apartment and I just don't feel it there. I'm an artist and I need inspiration. You can't just tell me to paint. Plus, he wants me to paint the mural I have on my living room wall in his bedroom and Truck would have a cow."

"I need to visit your apartment."

"Come by any time."

LATER THAT NIGHT...

After a relaxing day at home I find myself wanting to go to the club. First, I'm concerned about leaving Birdie alone, but that can't be an issue because she will be home alone when I go to work and honestly seems more capable of taking care of herself than I am. So, I dive head first into my closet and pull out the sexy dress Maddux told me not to wear. I slide out my panty drawer to grab the satin panties I prefer to wear with it and they're not where they belong. I always keep them in the front right corner of the drawer. When I unpacked that's where I put them. I remember it clearly. I spent the extra few minutes with the organizer in the drawer and put each of the panties in their own spot. Hot pink satin club panties in the front right corner which is now empty. "Where are they? Panties can't get up and walk away on their own. They need to be on me to get out!"

BIRDIE

I observe as my new servant has a fit about a missing pair of panties. Well, I believe stolen is the accurate term. I thought she was going out and I would finally get some alone time, but it seems the missing panties have thrown her into a tizzy and she's staying home. I don't know why. Panties seem extraneous and uncomfortable, I'd never wear them. I do, however, see myself enjoying some slumber in the middle of the big bed soon. Tomorrow I must figure out how to get her to clean my sand box. Servants do best when you teach them one task per day. All in time. She will be perfect.

CHAPTER SEVENTEEN

RAYE

*J*t's been a long relaxing Sunday and I started drinking early, polishing off the pitcher of sangria. It was the closest thing I had to mimosas for Sunday brunch, though it didn't go well with the peanut butter on my morning toaster waffle. It's kind of like super thin consistency jelly, so it should've gone with the peanut butter.

I've moved on to my friend Jack and we've been hanging out together all afternoon. Sipping and watching some of my favorite movies with some popcorn. I'm happy, or I should say happily drunk. I may go to bed early and I may eat every snack in my apartment. I need to go grocery shopping to stock up on snacks and my "J" friends. I start a grocery list when my doorbell buzzes. I stand to answer it and find it harder than I expected. I peek through the peephole and find Truck on the other side. I wonder what he wants? I've already decided I shouldn't be alone with him. The neighbor guy is simply too close and will end up awkward at every possible opportunity, but—he is hot and I would like to explore what's underneath those jeans. The bell buzzes again, oh yeah… he's at the door. I open the door and lean in the doorway, "Hey Truck."

"Hey Raye," he stops and seems unable to focus. "Umm, I decided I want to bake cookies. Do you have any sugar?"

He did not just ask me if I have any sugar. "I'm sugar through and through, baby." There's nothing sweeter than me.

Suddenly his lips are pressing against mine and he's pushing me backwards into my apartment. My door slams closed and his lips are asking for more. Out of breath he asks, "Why didn't you ask me in?"

"Did I need to?" I ask but he's already on to kissing my neck and nibbling my ear. This is a bad, bad idea and I'm in for it the whole way. He never answers me verbally. "Truck, condoms are in the left nightstand."

"I love a woman who's prepared," he holds me up against the wall in my living room on the way to my bedroom. His hands on my hips and creeping up my shirt on my bare skin until he finds my braless breasts and cups them, flicking my nipples.

I'm reminded I'm wearing my lazy Sunday clothes. This is not how I want Truck to find me. Baggy sweat pants, thread-bare t-shirt, and grey bikinis that say "Make Sunday your someday" across my butt and "Make a wish" on the front. Part of my days of the week panty collection. My hair is tied up lazy in a messy bun instead of down around my face the way it's cute. Not a drop of make up on my face.

He's in control. Moving us through my apartment. He pushes me down on my bed and grabs the elastic bottoms of my sweats at my ankles and yanks them off in one quick pull. Yes please! Wait, I need to play hard to get or something…

"What do you think you're doing?" I ask.

"Looking for your sugar. I think I know exactly where to find it," he says and skims his hands up my legs from my ankles to my thighs. Without hesitation he kisses my sex through my panties, "This smells sweet to me. I must be on the right path." He bites through the panties and rips them off of me with his teeth. Licking my seam up and down slowly, repeatedly. His hands firmly gripping my hips, he forces them wide with his head between my legs. "Definitely the sugar I was looking for." He drags his tongue deeper from the bottom to the top of me where he flattens his tongue against my clit and takes one slow lick. I reach for his head and thread my fingers through his mussed hair, tugging on it and holding him right where he is. He repeats the slow lick and I arch, pushing my center against his mouth. He groans and tickles my clit with the tip of his tongue increasing his speed at a torturing slow pace. I involuntarily squirm and buck into his mouth needing release. He intensifies the pressure of his tongue (currently my favorite thing about him and all I can imagine him as is a giant tongue) and my orgasm shatters me into a zillion pieces. Visions of Truck as this giant tongue floating in the stars and darkness of my mind's eye are all I have as I recover.

He grabs my feet and drags me to the edge of the bed. His arm wraps around my waist and flips me over, pulling my ass up into the air to a bent over position. The sound of the metallic wrapper ripping and his zipper leave me in anticipation of his next move. His mouth is on me again licking my scam and suddenly he shoves his huge hard cock into me. My head is up and back instantly, he grabs my hair and pulls my head back while he takes me. Smashing his rock-solid length into me mercilessly, over and over. His hands on my hips pulling my body to meet his strokes. He tightens his grasp, digging his fingers into my flesh. I'm hit by an unexpected orgasm—I never go twice—and scream out in pleasure.

"Fuck me," he grunts and collapses. Both of us lying cross ways on my bed and out of breath.

TRUCK

I wake in the middle of the night and I've got no clue where I am, but I'm not alone. I survey my surroundings without moving and find orange walls with a mural. Shit. I'm at Raye's. There's a blanket pulled over me and she's lying next to me. I reach down to rearrange myself and find the used condom still on my cock. Fuck me. What did I do! I'm also sated like never before. My memory kicks in, she went off and I came harder than I've ever come before. I've got to get out of here. I shouldn't have done this. I get up slowly, not wanting to wake her, and dispose of the used rubber. I pull my pants on and grab the tasty grey panties from the floor. I gaze at her, truly a gorgeous woman I can imagine as mine with explosive orgasms. It simply can't happen. I walk into the living room and the cat's sitting in front of the door with a judging stare. I approach the door and it doesn't move, just continues to glare at me. I attempt to pick it up and move it, but it simply walks out of my grasp and maintains its position. I remember how it rubbed on my legs and try a different tactic, scratching under its chin and behind its ears. It closes its eyes and I open the door only as much as necessary to get out before it changes its mind.

I quickly get into my apartment hoping nobody saw me. Grey panties still in my hand. Fuck! Vin will see that on the video footage of the hallway if he has to check it for any reason. I inhale a deep breath with her panties to my nose and crawl into my bed, ready for the repeat in my dreams.

BIRDIE

I must work on my ability to stand my ground and defend my home. This man is nothing short of a thief. First he forces his way in and takes advantage of my servant without asking me. I had plans for her. We were going to learn about the sand box. He should've at least requested permission before taking her when she was on duty. Now, I'm going to have to make note of what was done and where so I have a safe place to sleep in the bed. I don't understand this robber, why the panties when there are so many better options. Goodness, he could take me. I need to remember this. I must sharpen my claws in preparation. Though, it wouldn't be that bad. I'm not sure he's trainable like my current servant, but he has amazing hands and has obviously been trained in the art of feline Kama Sutra.

CHAPTER EIGHTEEN

RAYE

I get home from work and as I'm walking down the hall to my apartment I notice my door is open. My first thought is that Birdie figured out how to open the door and is gone, having decided that I'm not worthy. Then I realize she would have to be able to work the elevator or manage the heavy door to the stairwell, otherwise she's not leaving the fourth floor. I suppose she could be visiting a neighbor or could be held hostage. I walk faster as anxiety hits and I consider that there could be someone in my apartment right now shoving my belongings in their pockets and making notes to come back later for the bigger items.

I get to my apartment and peer in cautiously to find Vincent painting. I exhale and shed the tension. I walk in unsure of what to do or say. I suppose I did tell him he's always welcome. He is the property manager. "Hey Vincent."

"Hello! I hope you don't mind that I'm working on the

mural and steps. I had some time this afternoon and I like to get projects done. I hate having little things to do build up."

I take a deep breath remembering that he's the punisher, "It's fine. Though, it would've been nice to know before I about had a heart attack when I saw my door open."

"Oh! Sorry, I didn't think of that. I always leave the door open on any unit that I'm in. I've been keeping an eye on Birdie, she doesn't seem interested in leaving."

I gaze around and find her perched on the edge of the breakfast bar, observing happily. The steps are all mounted on the wall and he's adding blue sky and more detail to the tree. My furniture has been completely reconfigured and moved to the center of the room allowing easier access to all of the walls. I wonder which wall I will find him painting on next.

"As long as we're all safe that's all that matters. Changes and learning curves. We will get through it," I comment as my nerves calm.

"It appears someone had some fun last night," he glares at my bedroom. "I haven't seen a bed destroyed like that in a long time."

I follow his gaze and find the mattress and box spring no longer aligned, throw pillows fallen onto the floor and bedding a complete disaster. Note to self: consider making bed every morning. "Just me getting comfortable in my new surroundings. Trying to get the configuration of the pillows how I like and making a place for Birdie to nest."

"Try again," he says bluntly.

"I'm sorry?"

"There's a condom wrapper on the floor in there," Vincent points out.

Think fast, "That must have been here when I moved in."

He glares at me, "Who are you trying to pull a fast one on? I know a sex scene when I see it. Plus, I got a noise complaint from Cathy. The way she described it, I think she's jealous."

"Does that mean the punisher is going to come out?"

"Not for just one."

"Good to know."

"It could be interesting to find out who the guy was. I suppose I could go through the security footage, but that would take so much time," he nudges for details.

"Just a guy from the club," I lie.

"Interesting. For some reason I had an idea it was Truck," he pushes further.

"Why would you think that?"

"Those are the shoes he wears slid under your bed."

Fuck me. "Lots of men wear those shoes."

"Shall we inspect them, and see if they have the hole in them like Truck's?"

"Look, I made a mistake and I don't want to talk about it," I spit out quickly still not admitting it was Truck.

He closes the door, "Honey, Truck is no mistake."

"Yes it was a mistake. All I remember is that he knocked on my door drunk to ask for sugar and we ended up in my bed," I say exasperated and wishing I could remember the details.

"Tell me he's everything I've dreamed of," he begs.

"All I can tell you is I woke up more satisfied than I've ever been and I've got bruises on my hips."

"Show me."

"You're kidding, right?"

"We're just a couple of girls here. Show me."

"Why do you want to see that?"

"I want to know what kind of bruises. Is it like a full-on hand imprint bruise from a slap or spanking or fingerprint bruises or are you just sensitive like a peach?" He has spent way too much time thinking about this.

Reluctantly, I slide my leggings down on one side because he's piqued my interest and I need to investigate now too.

"Oh, those are fingerprint bruises on your hips. He must have had you doggy style and was really holding on," he surmises.

"Hello, my sex life not yours...."

He cuts me off. "It appears he was a bit rough, some bruising on your ass too. You lucky girl."

I could've told him that. There's a reason I wore leggings today. I'm sore and they're forgiving. "Is there anything else?"

"Yes, I'm going to need details next time. Please keep that in mind when you are self-medicating." He takes a step back from the wall and inspects his mural, "I think I'm going to leave the mural right there and let the paint dry. We will see if the color changes when it's completely dry and go from there. The paint around the steps should be dry enough not to get on Birdie."

"I won't show her until it's ready," I say.

"You act like you have a choice in the matter."

"I haven't shown her the cat bed or the cat tree and she hasn't paid attention to either of them," I state the facts.

"She's a cat. She either doesn't like them or isn't interested at the moment. It can change at any time. My grandmother had cats and they can be fickle creatures just like women."

"I suppose that means she's double trouble being a female cat," I ruminate.

"Time will tell. My work today is done, so I will leave you to enjoy your evening," he waves as he leaves and closes the door behind him.

I turn around and Birdie is sitting on the highest wall step gazing down at me. I swear that cat understands English.

I'VE NEVER HAD A CAT. She's done some weird shit. She digs in her poo box like she's trying to get through to the third floor. And now, she's running around my apartment like it's her own personal race track. I swear she's taking the curves on the walls! Why does she always do these things when I'm trying to sleep? And how does she change gears so quickly? What the fuck is this cat doing? Is she possessed? Then again, I'm quirky—we are perfect for each other.

BIRDIE

Run. Run. Faster. Faster. Climb the wall. I need to get it! I need to get it! Faster! Faster! Faster! Climb the wall. I can't get it. I'm going to get it. I can get it. I can get it! Faster. Faster. Faster! I need to get it! I'm speedway ready... zoom zoom zoom... Zoomies! Zoomies! Zoomies!

What's that light? Oooohhhh... red dot. Must kill the red dot. It must not beat me. I can get it. I must get it. I will win. The dot will not conquer me. How shiny! I'm going to get you red dot! Zoomies!

CHAPTER NINETEEN

RAYE

*J*t's been a long day, but I'm already out of snacks and can't survive another day without them. I rushed home from work to change into my jeans and check on Birdie. She can take care of herself, I'm simply not used to having a living creature in my apartment all of the time. I keep worrying about what I'm going to find when I get home. Will she eat something she shouldn't? Decide to scratch up my new furniture? Puke up a hairball on my rug? Pee on my bed? Get stuck on the top step and suddenly forget how to get down? You get the picture. All extremely unlikely things that I'm concerned about and that she is much too dignified for. Seriously, if there was a Venn diagram for me and Birdie the only things we would overlap on would be sleep, eat, nap, our apartment, and attraction to Truck.

I turn to lock the door behind me while I'm mentally reviewing the list of snacks I need: peanut butter, toaster waffles, salsa, tortilla chips, potato chips, candy, ice cream, canned whipped cream, popcorn, cheese powder, peanut butter cookies, chocolate chip cookies, wafer cookies, cheese, crackers, at least one of my "J" friends, and some frozen food... I don't cook. I need things I can toss in the microwave, preferably enchiladas, lasagna, cheesy potatoes—and none of those little individual meals, I want the family size one so I can have leftovers. I can handle preheating the oven and putting the meal in there as long as I set a timer. Trust me on this, I've turned casseroles into carbon. Oh, canned cinnamon rolls, I need those.

Out of nowhere I'm smashed into like I got run over by a truck and I'm about to fall on my ass, it's padded but it's still not a positive experience. Suddenly big hands are on me to keep me from hitting the ground and have me balanced back standing on two feet. Big hands are holding onto me by my hips. Big hands of the Truck that wasn't paying attention when he mowed into me. He squeezes my hips, using the tactic to pull me closer and hold me against him. Gazing into my eyes I witness his eyes go dark and hooded as he closes in on me and plants his lips on mine like I belong to him. I can't do this again. I try to keep my mind clear. I remember that we are on camera and Vincent or anyone else can go watch this whenever they want. He slides his finger along the waist band of my jeans and curls it around the string of the string bikinis I'm wearing. He tugs on it as he kisses me and has the string pulled three inches out of my jeans up my side. He slides his tongue into my mouth and I have flashbacks of how he used his tongue. I suck on his tongue and grab his ass with both hands. He yanks and rips my panties right off of me. I squeal more at the surprise of it than anything else.

I catch the pink and white cotton out of the corner of my eye and step away from him, "Those were my favorite panties! Jerk! Why'd you rip them off of me? They were perfectly comfortable and never ride up. They don't rub anywhere. They do their job and look cute doing it! Look at them!" He holds up the remnants of my white panties with the pink trim and a picture of a strawberry ice cream cone on the front with the words "lick me" printed across it. I stare him down, "You need to replace those."

"They're panties. I'm sure I can buy you a pair of panties."

"Not just any panties. Those are my favorite pair. They don't make that print anymore and they changed the pattern on the style. The new ones simply are not the same," I glare at him.

"I can't make last year's panties magically show up to purchase, that's simply not possible."

"Well, you will have to figure it out," I realize I've been yelling at him and hope I don't get another noise complaint. But this pisses me off! "Panties aren't free you know! I've already lost a couple pair when I moved somehow. When you find the panties buy me three!"

TRUCK

I have no idea how I'm supposed to handle this situation. Why did I rip the panties off of her? A question right up there with why did I take her panties that were hanging out of her drawer and why did I take the panties I ate off of her and why did I need to bite the panties right off of her and why can't I get her out of my head and why can't I get my other head to stop guiding me to her. Well, I did eat the one pair off of her so technically I think that pair is mine. I don't understand this level of crazy over a pair of panties.

There's got to be a way to diffuse this situation. I grin, "How about I make it up to you another way?" She glares at me waiting for an explanation and I show her the tip of my tongue.

"Do you think that makes everything better?" she asks sarcastically.

He raises his eyebrows, "It could."

She opens the door to her apartment and drags me in with her, slamming the door behind us. With no words we are back in her bedroom. No argument from me. The hips on this woman drive me insane. Something about her elicit curves with her creamy skin and angelic features has me hooked. She's a contradiction. Her soft sweet lips compared to how she uses them, and the words and sensual noises that come from her. She's good and bad in all the best ways. She's got her shoes kicked off and jeans flung to the other side of the room before I can get a condom out and accessible. I pin her to the wall, kissing her sweet lips and rubbing my needy cock against her. Her hands immediately squeeze between us to pull my belt off and unbutton my jeans. She grabs my cock with both hands and strokes it. I reach for the condom and give it to her to put on. Heated I lift her using the leverage of the wall and thrust into her hot wet pussy. She squeals at my intrusion and I want more. I stroke up into her hard and fast, the burn starts in my legs but it doesn't stop me. I wrap my arms around her waist, holding her on my cock. My fingers wrap around her hips and grip her tight, moving her on my cock. I'm worked up and want to blow my load. I toss her onto the bed and crawl up over her. I rub my aching cock against her heat and nibble on her neck. She arches into me and I want more, but she will always come first. I pull her shirt off and drag my tongue down her body, giving both of her perky pink nipples personal attention and an appreciative suck. Her wetness pushes me. I kiss each of her thighs and slide my tongue between her wet folds, lapping up her sweetness. My cock digging into the mattress. I can't wait. I move to her clit and blow on it before sucking it into my mouth. I release it and hold it between my lips while I work it with my tongue. Her body tightens beneath me and her moans are killing me. I lap at her with my flat tongue to get another taste of her and move the tip of my tongue across her clit quickly until she comes. Relentless, I continue my actions as she screams and pulls my hair. All that does is make me want more.

I flip her over flat on the bed and shove my cock back into her while I kiss her neck just behind her ear. She's tight and still contracting around me as I push and pull. I find myself biting her neck as I pound into her hard searching for my release. Fuck me she drives me crazy. She raises her ass in the air without prompting and I'm done instantly. This woman drains me. I crawl up next to her and pull her next to me.

BIRDIE

I've been staring at him for hours and he's still in my spot. It's time for me to be curled up on the bed. The spot by her feet is available, but I witnessed what happened there the other night and it is no longer a viable option. He's in the only acceptable spot, well, unless I climb up on top of the pillows. That would be soft and could be comfortable. I jump from my perch on the top of the cat tree to the bed, finding only enough room for the most agile of felines to land behind this man that keeps showing up and smells delightful. I sniff him as I walk the edge of the bed behind him and hop up onto the decorative pillows, a much better sleeping place than I'd anticipated. I dangle my luxurious tail in his face and swish it back and forth until he awakens, swatting my tail away in an extremely unacceptable manner. He sits up groggy and surveys the room before he gets up. He gets dressed and puts his shoes on, then reaches back to rub my chin and scratch behind my ears. I guess I'll excuse him for the unacceptable swat, or maybe get back at him for it later. He stands to go and curses under his breath as he grabs the shoes he left here the other night to take with him. I hope he enjoys the layer of my fur I've added to them, it's an upgrade to the ratty things. He's an odd character. He gets a grin on his face, picks up the ripped panties lying on the floor and stuffs them in his pocket. Should I wake my servant and alert her to this thief she keeps letting in? At this point they're trash, I'll let her sleep. I'm driven to jump down and guard the door so he can't leave, make it very clear who runs this place and how his thievery is not appreciated. But I'm comfortable and don't want to get up. I may not even jump down and take over my spot that he warmed for me...zzz.

RAYE

I have to quit waking up in the morning to a destroyed bedroom. I don't allow myself enough time in the morning to make my bed and clean up any details that may lead Detective Vincent down the "Did you have sex?" trail. I quickly throw the bed back together and kick the mattress and box spring into alignment. I do a floor check throughout my bedroom and under my bed—no wrappers of any kind lying on the floor and all shoes are gone. It's not perfect, but nothing beyond what Birdie does to the bed when she jumps on it and nests.

Plus, I still have no snacks and I'm out of toaster waffles. At least I have coffee. Unfortunately, as much as I've tried, I don't function without food to start my day. I search my kitchen while my coffee brews, and all I've got is the remains from Friday night—cold veggie sticks. Not what I consider breakfast or good with coffee, but it will have to do. I set the container on my counter to take with me and munch on my drive to work. Short on time, and I mean I will only be on time if I leave right now and the traffic lights are all in my favor, I grab my basic work uniform out of the closet and dress quickly, sliding into the easiest shoes possible on my way out the door.

Shit! I forgot I'm meeting Ashe for happy hour tonight.

CHAPTER TWENTY

RAYE

Ashley: Still on for happy hour?
Raye: Yes… meet at our place in 30 minutes?
Ashley: I'll be inside and have a table. Midge scheduled it so I could have some earlier free time.
Raye: I like this Midge more and more.
Ashley: Me, too. See you soon!

I walk into our favorite happy hour place and find Ashe sitting at a high-top with a view of the game and easy access to the bar. I'm sure it's intentional. I give her a hug and sit in the chair across from her.

"So, tell me how the new place is working out," she asks.

"I like it. I'm getting used to the new surroundings and Birdie. Vincent is cool in a 'one of the girls' way," I reply.

"What do you think about having a cat?"

"I didn't think I would, but I like it. It's weird that she's always there and you think she's sleeping but then she's right in front of you. We haven't had any issues."

"What's going on with Maddux?" Ashe asks while she sips a margarita.

"Nothing. I haven't heard a word from him," I think about it and find it odd that he hasn't called.

He doesn't really compare to Truck. Truck's no sugar daddy more of a fuck buddy, but that's what I thought Maddux was and he proposed so who the fuck knows? Damn Truck is fine though. His round ass and that strong cock... But his tongue, I'd make appointments for that treatment.

Ashe gazes around, "So, Truck?"

I straighten up, "What about him?"

"You were just talking about his cock and tongue... Did you two get to know each other better already?"

"Did I say that out loud?"

She nods, "But quietly. So that hickey came from Truck?"

I grasp my neck, one side and then the other, "What hickey?"

She reaches across the table and touches my neck, "That one." She touches my neck again, "And that one."

"I wasn't aware of any hickeys."

"Well, they're there."

"You'd think a co-worker would've said something."

"Were you running late this morning?" Ashe asks.

"Yeah, why?"

"Based on what you're wearing, it was either running late or you need to do laundry and you haven't been there long enough to run out of clean clothes yet."

"I'm not out of clothes yet, but I am out of snacks. I was going to restock last night when my plans got interrupted by a Truck."

"Tell me about it," Ashe says.

"I had to eat veggies with my coffee this morning because it was all I had left."

"I meant the Truck part," she chuckles. "Veggies with coffee is horrible." She picks up her phone and clicks away while she talks.

"Oh, he puts Maddux to shame. I can't tell you much about him though, so far he basically kisses me and we have sex."

"That's it?"

"There's nothing 'that's it' about having sex with that fine man. He gets me off first with his tongue. Gets me off again having sex. He doesn't just get up and leave, but he's gone before I wake up in the morning. He's perfect... except..." I decide to stop there.

"You can't leave me hanging with an 'except,' you have to give me more than that."

"He ripped my favorite panties last night."

"It's just a pair of panties."

"You would think, but I'm seeing a pattern."

"What do you mean?"

"The first time he ate my panties off of me."

"I'm sorry, what?"

"He bit right through them to get to my honey pot."

"So, you lose a pair of panties every time he comes over?"

I stop and consider what she said, "Interesting, my satin club panties went missing this weekend and he was over for the housewarming party. But, I wasn't wearing those, so I don't know what happened to those."

"So, you like this Truck guy?"

"He's attractive and good in bed."

"Sounds like a match," Ashe says excitedly.

"Hold on here, don't go getting any ideas. He's my neighbor and it needs to not happen again."

"You can always move if it goes bad, but what if he's the one? You have to give it a chance."

"What is there to give a chance? I open the door, he kisses me and we have sex. Boom. Boom. Bang!"

"There must be some discussion or something?"

"I yelled at him for ripping my panties off of me and he offered to make it up to me with his tongue. Does that count as discussion?"

"Technically yes, but no." She stops and I can see her wheels turning, "Maybe you should invite him over for dinner."

"I don't even have snacks and I can't cook."

"I ordered your snacks along with some other things and they will be at your door within the next hour. You can order take out and plate it like we did the hummus platter, just get rid of the packaging before he gets there. And maybe bake something so it smells good in your apartment and like something has been cooking to throw him off the take-out vibe."

"Did you order more peanut butter? Toaster waffles?"

"That's the part you're most concerned with?"

"I like food. I have a whole list of things, a can of those cinnamon rolls with the cream cheese frosting—I can make those."

"I know what you eat. I've been buying your groceries for years. You will be happy with the order," she chuckles. "You could bake biscuits from the can like the cinnamon rolls or crescent rolls and fill them with chocolate and top them with more chocolate."

"I'm sticking with the cinnamon rolls. I can do the tootsie roll when I meet him at the door, and isn't cinnamon an aphrodisiac or something like that?"

"So, are you going to invite him over and give the dinner thing a try?" Ashe asks.

"No."

"But you seem so into it."

"I'm into planning it with you, not actually doing it. I'm

keeping my neighbor sex visits exactly where they are and not screwing them up. I'm not taking any chances on losing that skillful tongue from my life." I stop and change the conversation before she can go any further. "Why were you asking about Maddux?"

"Oh," she stops and looks behind me, "he was sitting over there when you got here, but he's gone now. Are you done telling me about Truck?"

I smile at her and drink my margarita.

I GET HOME to boxes of groceries waiting at my door. My roommate curled up on my round chair bathing thoroughly. I watch her from across the room as I put my groceries away. She's sitting on her butt with her legs spread licking herself. I was just wishing Truck would show up at my door and do the same thing.

"Birdie, maybe you should do that in the other room. I do appreciate that you're not on the kitchen counter spread eagle."

BIRDIE

I do believe my servant is jealous of my self-sufficient skills and wishes she could lick herself like I lick myself. I've seen the chin scratcher here licking her twice now and I don't get it. It doesn't seem efficient. Am I missing the part where she provides him with instructions? I wouldn't trust him with my licking duties.

CHAPTER TWENTY-ONE

TRUCK

*T*his has to stop. She's just going to have to go. I can't get her out of my head and with her right next door there's always something reminding me of her. Her music playing, her door shutting, her panties in my pocket, her smell in my scruff, her patter when she walks through the building.

Truck: Are you in your office yet this morning?
Vincent: Of course. I'm always on time.
Truck: Can we have a meeting?
Vincent: Come on down. I've got the monthly numbers ready and waiting.

I'll go with that and bring up the problem when I get there. I put my t-shirt on and my San Diego Seals baseball cap because I'm not taking the time to check my hair. Fuck me if the elevator doesn't smell like her. I learned this lesson a long time ago. Don't get involved with chicks in the building.

I knock on the office door, "Good morning, Vincent."

"Good morning, Truck," he quirks his head. "Where'd you really get your name from?"

I chuckle, "Isn't it obvious? I'm built like one."

He sighs, "Try again."

Trying my hardest not to smile, "My parents met at a truck stop."

"Never mind. Let me go over the numbers with you," he stops and opens a folder. "We are currently at capacity. The expenses involved getting the last tenant onboarded included paint, cleaning crew, and minor repairs that I handled in last month's budget. Including the backsplash project I added and the tree mural supplies the total cost not including my time that you would have to pay for anyway came to a total of $712. I was able to handle most of the labor myself," Vin closed the folder as if the discussion was over.

"Tree mural?"

"Yes, didn't you see it when you were over there having sex?" Vin inquires.

Ummm, "What?"

"I know you have already been there and done the deed. I've been trying to get you for years. She's only been here a week," Vin glares at me.

"First, we are friends and you are my employee, and you know I'm not into dudes that way. It has nothing to do with you, it's all me and the fact that I'm attracted to women not men. I'm sorry. Again, it's me and not you." Why does this seem like a break up conversation? I gaze at him waiting for confirmation.

Vin holds his head up tall, "Continue."

"Second, why would you think I've already had sex with her?" I'm curious where this came from.

Vin glares at me again, "Your shoes were in her bedroom and before you try to tell me that you were helping her do something, the condom wrapper was on the floor. Don't even try to tell me you were blowing up balloons or jumping on the bed or any other lame excuse."

"Anyway, she has to go," I'm not responding to any of the rest of it.

"I disagree. She's the perfect addition to the community," Vin replies.

"She has a pet and pets must be pre-approved. Kick her out," I suggest.

"I pre-approved the cat," he replies.

"How did she get the cat pre-approved if she didn't know Ashe was bringing it to her?"

"Ashe got Birdie pre-approved. There you have it. She stays," Vin states, case closed.

"There's got to be something, figure it out and get her out."

"Well, there have been two noise complaints from Cathy. But I didn't take them seriously," Vin hem-haws.

"A complaint should always be taken serious. We don't need any drama around here."

Vin smirks, "Cathy seemed to be enjoying telling me the story about the noise both times a bit too much and in detail. She was extremely clear that the noise was a couple having sex and it was a new sound in the building so she's confident it's Raye and some guy visiting her." He glares at me hard. "Honestly, she told a story that was more about jealousy than inappropriate noise and it left me imagining her with a glass to the wall so she could hear all the details."

Vin continues, "Plus, it's only two complaints and they are from the same tenant. It's not enough to evict her."

"It's a start. I trust that you will find a way," I smile.

Vin relaxes back in his chair, "May we have a discussion off the record?"

I don't have a choice, "Sure."

"Why is it that you want her gone? You know, there's

nothing wrong with you being attracted to a woman or a man. You deserve happiness and for many that's getting coupled. She's a beautiful woman who I'm going to assume is interested in you since you've fornicated multiple times. I'm spitballing here, but have you considered asking her out? You wait much longer and you're going to turn into an old man and you won't be able to join the rest of the people who populate the world because your sperm will be too slow. A gorgeous young woman like that would be perfect for you and could help you in and out of your wheel chair as you get older. You're creeping up on 50 right?" He smiles.

"Off the record?" I confirm.

"Yes, of course," he agrees.

"You are an asshole and you know exactly how old I am. You picked that girl on purpose because she's the right age for me," I stand and lean on the front of his desk.

"It's all possible hypothesis, but how do I know how old you are? It could be fabricated like your name."

I glare at him, "My name is Truck."

"Right, right. And I suppose that's a family name?"

I gaze back at him as I leave his office, "I'm rugged enough to handle any obstacle."

"If that's the case, there's an obstacle living next door to you," he yells after me and I flip him the bird.

Vincent: I'm here if you need help getting your mind off of her.
Truck: Thanks for that.
Vincent: Always happy to help *kisses*

CHAPTER TWENTY-TWO

RAYE

I get home from the bar to find bags of groceries sitting on my doorstep. Everything I was planning to get and more, some actual real food and frozen microwave meals. Ashe knows how to take care of me. Why couldn't she have been born with a cock?

> Raye: Thank you… you know me too well.
> Ashley: You're welcome.
> Ashley: I'll send you the link to your account so all you have to do is order and you can click reorder next to things you've ordered before—like everything I ordered tonight.
> Raye: I can do this. Much easier not to go to the store.
> Ashley: Yea, except you miss out on new stuff and impulse buys.

There's a knock on my door.

Raye: Gotta go… someone's at my door.

Ashley: I hope it's Truck!

Ashley: Maybe you'll get knocked up too.

Raye: SHUT UP!

I peep through the hole and find Maddux standing there. What the hell does he want? How does he even know where I live? Can I just ignore him and leave him standing there?

"I can see you looking at me through the peephole," he says in an irritated voice.

Shit. I open the door with a fake smile on my face, "Hey, how are you doing?"

He steps forward like he's going to walk right in and I lean on the door jamb, filling the space as best I can to block him.

He glares at me, "Let me in."

"I'm not comfortable with that," I state matter-of-factly.

He sighs, exasperated, "I understand now, you weren't prepared for me to propose. I caught you off guard, my flower."

I stare at him silently.

"Now I have found you and everything will be better. You can tell me you made a mistake and accept my proposal," he smiles like a conceited ass.

I glare at him, "How did you find me?"

"How doesn't matter, all that matters is that I found you," he places his hand over his heart.

"How matters to me," I reply sternly.

"I saw your car parked outside," he replies vaguely.

"And that was enough for you to find me in the middle on the fourth floor?" I question sarcastically.

"I saw your name on the address box," he grins and gazes to the side.

"That's interesting because my name isn't on the address boxes yet. Why don't you try the truth? I didn't make a mistake and I'm not changing my mind for a liar," my voice gets louder with every word.

He grits his teeth, "I followed you from the bar."

I should've known, "Ashe told me you were there and you left before us. Tell me you're not such a loser who would wait in his car, hiding so he could follow a woman home."

"Just let me come in and we can discuss this, baby. This is not a hallway discussion for your neighbors to take part in," he demands.

"What part of this do you not understand? I'm not your baby. If I wanted to see you I would've given you my address," I reply.

"Why are you talking to me like this? Where did this attitude come from?" Speaking to me like I'm a child.

"This is who I am. If you don't know that, then you don't know me at all," I refuse to back down.

He steps forward, trying to push his way in.

"You don't know me at all! Leave me alone!" I yell at him and shove him back. I step inside quickly and turn to close the door, but he grabs me by the hair. I make fists and swing around wildly, "You loser ass, self-centered, selfish, show off, couldn't get a woman if you weren't a sugar daddy fucking old man with an inadequate dick." I connect, slugging him in the face. He falls back and I quickly go inside and slam the door shut, latching the locks.

Less than a minute later, he's pounding on my door, "Raye! I know you don't mean those things. Let me in! Please! Raye!" He stops and continues, "Please, baby! I love you. Marry me and I'll do anything for you. I'll give you everything. We belong together."

"This is my place, not yours. You don't get to call the shots and I'm not interested! You don't know what love is! You think you can pay for everything," I yell back at him through the door. "You can't pay for me."

His tone changes to the true ass that he is, "Whatever you meaningless piece of trash. You're just a slutty bitch anyway."

"You know I'm a ho—I was with you!" I call back at him.

I peep through the door and he's still standing there. He can stand there all night for all I care.

I turn to go back to the kitchen and Birdie is sitting there in the middle of the living room, "Where were you on that one? Aren't you supposed to be my wing girl? I've seen you sharpening those claws of yours. It would've been an opportunity to use them."

She simply walks over to me and figure eights between my legs multiple times until I pet her head.

"Is this how you tell me I did a good job or the right thing?" I ask as I scratch under her chin.

She purrs and falls to the floor, rolling over to expose her belly. I rub her belly a few times and she pops up, glares at me and walks away. I don't understand cats.

BIRDIE

I think my servant handled that well, keeping the crazy person out of our domain and keeping me safe. I'm adding claw training to her list of things to learn. I believe it would've been very helpful during the scuffle they had and more effective than the attempt at some sort of boxing. In addition we need to work on understanding limits. Rolling over on my back doesn't mean you are invited to touch my underside, especially not repeatedly. It's like stroking my tail, don't do it more than once. She did pass the figure eight trip attempt test, oddly I think she enjoyed it.

CHAPTER TWENTY-THREE

TRUCK

*W*hy is my phone ringing? It's too early for this. I force my eyes open and reach for my phone, "Hello?"

"Good morning. We have an issue. Please join me in my office at your soonest convenience," Vincent is too fast-paced for this time of morning.

"Okay. I'm not awake yet, I'll be there soon," I reply groggily.

"No problem. Bring coffee and donuts. We are going to need them," He hangs up.

This can't be good. I need to talk to Vin after what I saw last night anyway. I might as well get it over with. I roll over and my morning surf report is telling me to grab my board and go, but that's not going to happen. I get up and shower, trying to clear my head for the day. I close my eyes and let the water fall over me, and all I can think about is Raye.

I pulled the security footage up last night when I heard her door slam. She's trouble in more ways than one. Her drama doesn't belong in my building. The other tenants are all quiet and settled, it's been a half dozen years or so since we've seen an incident like this.

The part that's sticking with me is how fiery she is. That woman is becoming harder and harder to ignore. She's perfect for me. She handles business and isn't afraid to stand up for herself. Plus, she has her own set of morals and she sticks to them. Anyone would be lucky to have her as a friend and that mother fucker who was here last night doesn't deserve to be anywhere near her. I want to find him and beat him into oblivion. Another reason she needs to go, he will come back and I'm not going to let this go. How dare he pull on that beautiful woman's hair and treat her so disrespectfully. Nobody should get treated that way, especially not a woman as radiant as Raye.

I get out of the shower ticked off and usually it has the opposite effect. I get dressed quickly and run my fingers through my wet hair. I take the stairs down the back way and go next door to pick up coffee and donuts, that's what Vin was really asking for. I do what I can to keep him happy, he's integrated himself so thoroughly that I wouldn't know what to do without him and I'm okay with that.

I walk into the donut shop, "Good morning, Jodi,"

"Hey Truck, Vincent told me you were coming," she gathers a carrier with coffee and donuts she has ready to go. "Any special requests today?"

"Extra donut holes and one of those cake donuts with the chocolate frosting and peanuts on it please," I smile at her.

She giggles, "Already covered, honey." She hands me the carrier, "I'll be here if you need anything else."

"Thanks, babe," I call back over my shoulder. The order is heavier than usual and we're having large coffees, it must be bad.

I walk into the office and set the carrier on his desk. "I have something I need to discuss with you, too. So, who's first?"

"Well, good morning Mr. Grumpy. It's nice to see you, too," he smiles at me. "Business always comes first. Is your conversation business?"

I stop and consider his question. If I beat the guy to a pulp and we get sued or I go to jail, it would have an impact on business, "It is regarding something that will impact the building and possibly your paycheck."

Vin grabs a coffee, "You first."

"I heard a door slam on my floor last night so I checked the security footage…" Vin cuts me off.

"My discussion is about that as well, I've already reviewed the footage. What do we do?"

"If that man sets foot in this building again I'm going to show him what it's like to get run over by a truck. There's no reason anyone should get treated like that, especially not my girl. He was a raging asshole. I love that she was fierce and stood up for herself."

Vin glares at me wide-eyed, "Okay. We have different issues with the same problem."

"How's that?" I ask not understanding how anything is more important than what I said.

"Are you aware that you just referred to Raye as your girl?" Vin asks in a calm tone and sips his coffee.

"I did not," I state unwavering.

"You did and it goes right along with the fact that you want to defend her, so think about it for a minute. It's okay. Have a seat," Vin gets up and walks around behind me, closing the office door and leading me to sit. He pats me on the shoulder, "It'll be okay. I'm here to help. Eat a donut hole and drink some of your coffee. Breathe." He pops three donut holes in his mouth one right after the other. He never does that. He only eats one. "Why do you have to make my job so complicated?"

I open my mouth to defend myself and Vin puts his hand up, "That was rhetorical." He gets a notepad and starts to make notes, "Let me get this all straight and we will find a solution to all of it. You are in love with Raye and you probably haven't told her."

"Hold on. I'm not in love with anybody."

"Okay, in order to proceed with this conversation, let's say you are interested in Raye. Fair?" Vin stares at me waiting for me to respond.

Am I interested in Raye? I want to beat that guy and I can't stop thinking about her. She's perfect for me. Fuck! I am in love with her, damn it! "Sure, I guess."

"Now we are starting to get somewhere, how does your problem affect the building?"

"When that asshole sues me and the building, and I end up in jail for attempted manslaughter, it could impact the building," I say calmly with a sarcastic smile on my face and shove a couple donut holes in my mouth.

"Okay, noted. Are you ready for my issue?" He asks politely.

"Sure, why not," I lean my head back and stare at the ceiling.

"I had four complaints about Raye this morning. All from different tenants and based on the security footage all valid. I understand it wasn't necessarily her fault, but we can't have that. I have to evict her. It's just business. I hate it, she's fabulous and I wish there was another way," Vin states factually.

"What were the complaints?" I ask though I'm not sure why. I saw all of it.

Vin opens her file, "In addition to the two complaints about sex noise from Cathy, we have a complaint about yelling in the hall, a complaint about causing a ruckus, a complaint about noise after acceptable hours, and two complaints about door slamming and violence. All different tenants except Cathy complained about the door slamming, too."

He stops and stares at me.

"There's got to be a way to fix this," I say.

"You were the first one who wanted her gone. I can do that now with no problem. There are too many complaints to ignore them. She has to go."

"I understand, do what you need to do. What about the guy? How do we keep him away from here?"

He cocks his head, "I'd assume he won't be a problem if she's not here."

"But, what if she is or visits? Or what if I find a way she can stay?" I want a different solution. Anything to keep her here.

Vin sits back in his chair, "I may be able to handle that."

"Good. Do what you need to do. Evict her," I say the words and hate it.

"Are you sure about this?" Vin asks.

"It's business and there's no way around it," I state and leave taking the rest of the donuts with me.

CHAPTER TWENTY-FOUR

RAYE

I get home from work to find an envelope taped to my door that says "I'm sorry. This is all business. Don't hate me." on it. What the hell? I go inside and open it to find an eviction notice. "Are you fucking kidding me right now? I just got moved in!" I read further about the complaints and I can't argue any of them. Except it takes two for the sex noises and Maddux will never be back. I hope Maddux doesn't come back. I guess he could. Can't blame a man for being unable to stay away from me.

I stare at Birdie sitting on the breakfast bar, "What do you think about this? We are being evicted. Now I have to find a new place and they have to accept pets! Where are we going to go? I'm not going back to Maddux. There's no fucking way that's happening. This place is perfect! I don't want to move! It's all his fault! Why did he have to come over here? I hope I never see him again. What are we going to do?"

Birdie jumps down and stands with her butt to me and her

tail in the air. She walks toward the kitchen and turns to make sure I'm paying attention. I follow her and she hops back up on the counter, pawing at the container with her treats in it. I step up next to the counter and she headbutts my arm. I get her a treat and set it on the counter for her, but she doesn't eat it. She turns back to me and paws at my belly. I grab a bag of chips and open it, and she eats her treat. "You think we need to have snack? Cat, are you a comfort eater like me?" I put a bag of popcorn in the microwave and try to figure out what I'm going to do.

BIRDIE

I'm beginning to wonder if my servant is a lunatic. It's one thing that she talks to me and completely another that she talks to the empty space around her. I'm concerned that she's seeing things that aren't there or talking to imaginary friends. She's always upset or frustrated when she does this. I suppose I would be too if I was talking to someone and they refused to respond. I'm hoping a snack will settle her down, like it does for me. I will sit nearby and observe her, she needs a keeper more than I do. She's staring at me, "You need to stop judging me. I'm the one with the thumbs who opens your food." I wash my face and change positions so I can lick myself. She's glaring at me now, "That's just showing off!" I may not be safe here. I make my way to the top step, she can't reach me here.

RAYE

I need my bestie, I call Ashe.

"Helloooooo!" She says obviously in a good mood.

"Hi, do you know how much I love and adore you?" I ask in as positive a tone as I can muster.

"Uh oh, what's wrong?"

"I'm getting evicted," I state deadpan.

"Are you kidding?"

"I wish I was."

"You just moved there."

"You're telling me?"

"Can they do that? Did they give you a reason?"

"Other tenants have complained about me too many times apparently." This is when I realize I haven't talked to Ashe since Maddux was here. Everything bad is his fault. "Maddux showed up here last night and it didn't go well."

"What are the complaints?"

"Noise, yelling, door slamming, causing a ruckus, violence and a couple complaints from the days before I already knew about but Vincent wasn't taking seriously. I'm guessing he couldn't ignore them when he got others."

"Did those things happen?"

"It wasn't good. I'm not going to lie. I didn't let him in and there was a scuffle."

"Are you okay?"

"No. I don't want to move. I like it here," I whine.

"Maybe I can have a property manager to property manager conversation with Vincent and fix it?"

"I was thinking I should take you up on the unit with the beach view. It's going to be even harder to find a place that allows pets."

She sighs, "I rented that unit out when you got moved in."

Of course she did. It's in a great building. "Do you have anything else?"

"The only thing I have available is too far from me."

"How far?"

"Hawaii."

"That would be a difficult work commute."

"It would. You can always move back here and wait for the next unit to open up."

"I can't do that. I made the step to have my own place and I need to stick to it."

"At least it's an option."

"I'll keep it in mind. I may not have a choice."

There's a knock on my door again and I'm dreading it. I peek through the peep hole to find Truck.

"I have to go, Truck is at the door."

"Text me later, bye."

I open the door, "What's up?"

"I saw the envelope on your door earlier and thought you might like to get out for a bit," no funny grin, just a kind heart.

"So, you know?"

"I've seen the envelopes before. There's one that's 'you're in trouble' and there's one that's 'get out.' I'm sorry you have to go."

"I don't want to go anywhere, but you are welcome to come in," I move out of his way and gesture to the inside.

"I thought you might say that," he turns to the side and picks up a couple bags before he walks in.

He kisses my cheek as he walks in and sits in my round chair. Damn he smells good. On top of everything else, I have to leave my position as his neighbor and some other woman is probably going to move in and get to take advantage of his talented tongue. He takes a bottle of Jack out of one of the bags and sets it on the table. Imagine that, we have a "J" friend in common. He rips the other bag open creating a paper bag bowl, and it's full of donut holes. I grab two shot glasses from the cabinet and sit on my couch.

He pats the chair next to him, "You are way too far over there to be passing this bottle back and forth."

I move over next to him and he fills the shot glasses and hands one to me. He clinks his against mine, "Cheers." We both throw a shot back. "Have you had a chance to try the donuts from next door yet?"

"No, and I don't want to try something else I'm going to be missing out on."

He shakes his head, "You've got to." He picks one up and shoves it in my mouth whole.

I can't help but smile as I try to see the whole thing in my mouth and not spray crumbs all over my living room. "Oh my, those are light and decadent at the same time," I swallow and try another.

He pours more shots and toasts again, "To new friends." We throw the shots back and he pours more as I wander to my kitchen and pull the bag of popcorn from the microwave. I sit back down next to him and he wraps his arms around me giving me a hug. I rip the popcorn bag the same way as the donut holes and set it on the table. "Ah, salty to go with the sweet," he says and laughs. "Your turn to toast," he says and grabs a handful of popcorn.

I pick up my shot glass and try to be clever, "To salty and sweet and what happens when they come together."

He sets his glass down and gazes into my eyes, different than he has ever before. He takes my glass from me and kisses me like he could kiss me for hours. Not a come fuck me kiss. He pulls away and smiles. We do our shots and he feeds me another donut hole. Before I can swallow, he's kissing me again and has his arms wrapped around me like maybe he doesn't want me to leave.

CHAPTER TWENTY-FIVE

TRUCK

I should never have gone to Raye's. I woke up in her bed with her the next morning and we didn't have sex. What was I thinking? Always get laid and get out when they're sleeping. Kissing her was the wrong move, too. It made everything worse. It changed from sex to, well, I don't know what. That was a week ago. I've been avoiding her ever since.

Vincent: What day of the Raye embargo is it?

Truck: Why do you have to remind me of her?

Truck: You have texted me that same question every day.

Truck: You know the answer.

Vincent: Can you clarify for me?

Vincent: Are we counting from the last time you had sex with her or the night you stayed over?

Vincent: You're always welcome at my apartment, if you need a friend.

Truck: Have you talked to her?

Vincent: Not much. She's having a hard time finding a place.

Truck: We did what we had to do, right?

Vincent: Yes. It's business.

RAYE

I don't get it. My new "friend" evicts me. My hot neighbor shows up to console me and doesn't get naked. And, when my girl brain gets the idea that he's interested in being more than a booty call—he's gone. Well, he's not gone. He's on the other side of my living room wall, right here in the apartment next door. I'd at least run into him every day since I moved in, but not so much as a sighting across the parking lot in the last week. Did I do something wrong? Okay, I got evicted for basically disturbing the peace, but that wasn't only me. There was always someone else involved and Maddux was only here once. Truck is just as responsible for two of the complaints as I am, he just slipped under the radar and wasn't a named offender.

The worst part? I loved hanging out with him with my clothes on. Don't get me wrong, I loved everything about the naked times and that man has skills. I've never fancied spending time with men. Take the sex, maybe a meal, dance for hours, and run. It checks all the boxes for a sugar daddy and makes sense why I'm attracted to them. It's how I operate. I did have my Maddux Phase, but it was short-lived and I can't figure out what I saw in him. That's not true, I enjoyed how he acted like my sugar daddy. It was fun. The problem with that is sugar daddies are temporary and not meant to be a partner, which his actions made extremely clear over the last few weeks. The time I've had alone has had me thinking—I want more. But, until more comes my way, I'm not turning down a skillful booty call. There's no reason to stay home at night pining after a man that may not exist. Ashe said it best, "women have needs" and I'm taking a lesson from her because I don't want those "needs" to get me pregnant like they did her. I'm not ready for that and I may never be. I thought I was taking a big step with a plant, and sometimes I wonder if the cat is actually taking care of me.

Truck? He's different. He didn't try to whisk me off of my feet to some fancy pants restaurant. He didn't even ask me out to dinner. He showed up at my door and kissed me. He showed up at my door with Jack and donuts because I needed a friend. I've not witnessed a pretentious bone in his body. I'm surprised he doesn't wander around barefoot and shirtless. I'd admire that view, might snap a couple photos without his knowledge to keep for later. He's down to earth and not trying to impress anyone. It captivates me how a man with his natural charm and undeniably handsome appearance (cheekbones like that) is ambivalent to the numerous women around him who must be attracted to him. Maybe that's it. Maybe he has multiple women. Maybe his girlfriend was on vacation and he used me to fill in the gap. As much as I don't trust men, I can't believe that would be Truck. None of it matters, I'm not going to be that woman who knocks on his door. Or is it my turn? He came to me a few times and I didn't go to him. Could it hurt? I'm leaving anyway.

TRUCK

> Vincent: Do you realize you haven't been outside in ten days?
> Truck: That's not true. I've been surfing and I picked up from Jodi.
> Vincent: You haven't been out of the building during my work hours.
> Truck: I've been home from surfing before you start your work day.
> Vincent: Barring the occasional exceptional surf days, since when are you out of bed before 9am?
> Truck: I changed my pattern up, trying to get out when the surf is best.
> Vincent: Does that require you to be home, locked in your apartment before 8am on weekdays?
> Truck: I suppose that could be when the waves are rockin'.
> Vincent: Could it also be the earliest a certain straw-berry blond leaves for work in the morning?
> Truck: I have no idea what you are talking about.
> Vincent: Day 10, Truck.

It's one o'clock in the afternoon and I hear Raye's door. I peek out the door to find her there with empty boxes and she catches me. Staring straight at me with my door cracked open less than an inch, "Hey." Her voice without any energy and no radiance beaming from her.

Closing the door quickly will simply make it more obvious that I was spying on her. As much as I should keep my distance, I don't want to. No smile on her face is unacceptable. I open the door and walk out into the hallway, letting it close behind me. "Hey."

She flashes a fake smile at me, "Alright then, I've got to go."

She pushes her door open and as she's walking inside I spill words without thought, "So, would you like to have dinner at my place tonight? Maybe watch a movie?" Torture myself for 10 days and now I fuck it all up. I swear I notice the security camera move, Vincent for sure saw her come in. I bet he's zooming in to watch. Why do I have all this time to think? She's staring at me and not responding. This can't be good. Women always have something to say. Maybe she didn't hear me. "So? Are you busy tonight?" I smile trying to break the icy conversation, and lean against the wall hoping I come off nonchalant. I notice a new security camera has been installed across the hall from my door, it's focused on my door and Raye's which are separated by about four inches of drywall.

Vincent: Tell her she's beautiful.
Vincent: Tell her that you are an ass.
Vincent: Tell her that her eyes remind you of the ocean and you want to dive right in.
Vincent: Tell her you miss her.

She gazes at the phone in my hand that keeps going off on rapid fire, "I think you have other business to tend to."

"What do you mean?"

"I'm not here to fill in when your other women aren't

available for you. I'm not a side piece. You've got plenty to handle and don't need me."

I hold my phone up, "This is Vincent."

"Well, whatever your preference is doesn't matter," she shakes her head. "He's a very attractive man."

"Wait. No, no, no. I'm not into dudes and there are no other chicks."

"Do you think I'm an idiot? Have you looked in the mirror?" She chuckles insincerely and her eyebrows furrow.

I run my fingers through my hair, "Do you want to have dinner with me tonight or not?"

"I guess. Where are you taking me?"

"Nowhere, just come over. I've got it handled," I grin. "Is there anything you don't like? You eat steak?"

"I'm not a fan of seafood. Steak is good. What time?"

"Will six work?"

She nods, "I'm supposed to be packing tonight."

"It can wait," I say confidently.

She glares at me, "From the mouth of a man who has a place to live." She opens her door and shuts it behind her as she walks into her apartment.

Vincent: From the smile on your face I'm going to say she said yes.

Truck: Why is there a new security camera focused on my door?

Vincent: There's not.

Truck: Then what am I looking at?

Vincent: A new security camera focused on Raye's door for the safety of the community and documentation of any future complaints.

Truck: This camera seems to have more functions than the others.

Vincent: Of course. It's the new model.

Truck: How much did it cost me?

Vincent: Stop worrying about everything. I've got it handled.

Truck: Does it have zoom?

Truck: I know I saw it move.

Vincent: I didn't splurge. I stuck to the 1080p and 30fps.

Truck: A security camera in a hallway that's eight feet wide doesn't need to be 1080p or 30fps.

Truck: It's a security camera. You're not making your YouTube videos and TikTok reels with it.

Vincent: Imagine the footage I could capture.

Vincent: It has 130-degree field of view, I didn't go super wide angle.

Truck: Tell me about the zoom.

Vincent: It's necessary for the safety of the building and our tenants.

Truck: How far can you zoom in?

Vincent: You really need to use those blackhead removing pore strips I put in your stocking for Christmas.

Shit! One more thing I need to do before dinner.

I open my refrigerator and pantry, searching for what's on tonight's menu. I'm not a chef by any means, but I do know my way around the kitchen. I want steak, but the morning shows have all been about what to do with spaghetti this week.

I put my Seals baseball cap on, grab my keys and wallet, and head out the door after my ingredients.

CHAPTER TWENTY-SIX

RAYE

*W*hy did I agree to go to his place? It's better than packing. He's no sugar daddy, but he checks a couple boxes off of my list—a meal and possibly some skilled naked time, and I'm not over the view of his hot ass.

I'm catching up on laundry today, so I can start packing and be ready if I ever find a place. I thought it was difficult before, well add Birdie to the mix and there's less options plus higher rent. They want monthly rent for the cat! She doesn't take up any more space. It's not like they add on a room for her or anything. I'm the one giving up square footage to her cat tree and part of my view to her window hammock, though I've never seen her use either one of them.

Huh, where is she? I've been home for ten minutes and she's not in my face. It's 2 o'clock in the afternoon. Why isn't she up bathing or doing her yoga or whatever cats do? "Birdie?"

She's not on the bed. She's not sitting on the kitchen

counter next to my coffeemaker. She's not eating or drinking. She's not glaring at me judgingly from the breakfast bar. She's not curled up in my round chair. She's not in her cat bad. She's not in the cat tree. She's not in her hammock. She's not in the cat box. This is only a one-bedroom apartment, where is she?

I turn and pick up the boxes I left by the door to hide them in the bedroom while I continue my search for Birdie, and wonder why they seem heavier as Birdie sits up in the box and puts her nose against mine, tickling me with her whiskers. She's not a fan of being picked up, so this is different. She yawns and curls up in a ball in the bottom of the box. I put the boxes back down. This is not conducive to packing. Maybe Birdie has the right idea. I start my laundry and find myself a cat nap.

THE DRYER BUZZER wakes me up. It's warm lying in my bed with the sun shining in during the afternoon. I sit up ready to tend to the laundry and Birdie lifts her head, stands up, and stretches from where she had been sleeping next to me. Staring at me, she climbs into my lap and puts her front paws up on my chest until I lie back down. I'm not arguing with her. Apparently it's still nap time and she's purring while she curls up on top of me. I told you she's the one taking care of me.

I WAKE up to the sun going down and my phone rings as if she had been watching and waiting for me to open my eyes, "Hey Ashe."

"Hi, how's packing going?" She asks cheerily.

"I'm getting laundry caught up and bonding with Birdie."

"Bonding with the cat?"

"Yea, she's a decent roommate most of the time. Other than when she makes noise at night."

"So, what are you two doing?" Ashe asks curiously.

"Birdie climbed into my moving boxes and then suggested a cat nap."

"I suppose you have time to pack tonight. Did you find a place yet?"

"No, and I have plans tonight."

"Plans? You have a date or something with Birdie?"

"First, watch yourself. Birdie would be offended. And I don't know if I'd call it a date."

"Are you going out?"

"No, just next door."

"Wait. I thought you said he disappeared."

"I didn't see or hear anything from him for over a week."

"And now he's suddenly back in our lives? I'm going to need more information."

Of course she is, "Well, I'll provide that information after I go to his place for dinner tonight. I have to hurry and get ready. My cat nap was longer than I thought."

"Interesting."

"He swears I'm the only woman and I told him I'm not a side piece."

"I'm sorry, is this my best friend Raye?"

"I know! What was I saying? Why was he defending it? I may lock the door and stay home. Now I need to find a place and move for more reasons than one," I rant.

"You like him!" she exclaims and laughs.

"He is a fine piece of man, but I'm not going there." I continue my inner thoughts out loud, "If only my girl brain didn't get the stupid idea that he wants more than sex."

"Wait. What?" Her voice drops an octave.

"I've gotta go get ready. Talk tomorrow." I hang up quickly, not ready to have that conversation.

Ashley: You can't drop a bomb like that and hang up on me.
Ashley: When did you get a girl brain?
Ashley: Why do you think he wants more than sex?
Ashley: What am I missing here?
Ashley: I don't like not living with you.
Ashley: You hide things from me.
Raye: Says the woman who ran away and hid she was pregnant from me.
Ashley: That may not have been the best thing to do.
Raye: Trust Fund Baby
Ashley: I wasn't hiding from you and I needed time.
Raye: I'm over it now.
Raye: I gotta go!
Ashley: I'm not done!
Ashley: What aren't you telling me?
Ashley: RAYE!

I turn my sound off and toss my phone on my bed, while I get ready to go to Truck's. I check the mirror as I decide what to wear. I've got a line on my face from where it was planted on the seam of my pillowcase and my hair is flat on one side. I grab a dress out of my closet and put it back, it's not that kind of night. I dig my favorite shorts and tank top combo out of my dresser and lay them out on my bed.

I turn the shower on and indulge myself in the hot steam. Hopefully it steams the crease out of my face. My hair will be a whole other issue. It's invigorating to scrub everything away and clear my head. I wrap a towel around my body and tie my wet hair up into a messy knot with stray curls sticking out of it.

I check the mirror and the crease is gone. My bathroom is a bomb of fabulously fresh and fruity scents.

I emerge a new woman, refreshed and ready to have dinner with my neighbor—which is exactly what this is—dinner and maybe watch a movie with my neighbor. My neighbor who brought Jack and donuts over to hang out and console me when I got my eviction notice. My neighbor who has shown up at my door drunk and kissed me. My neighbor who ripped my panties right off of my body. My neighbor who bit my panties off of me with his teeth. My neighbor who kisses like he wants more.

I walk into my bedroom to find Birdie sitting on the clothes I have waiting for me on my bed and realize she's right, it's not the right outfit. I pull my turquoise above the knee length, soft cotton sundress with ties at the shoulders over my head. It's simple yet flatteringly skims my features. I step into my slides and turn around to find Birdie gazing up at me from her position sitting in the middle of the doorway.

I bend down and pet her chin, "Is this better?"

She purrs instantly and licks my hand.

"I'll take that as a yes," and wonder when I went full on cat lady. Then a crazy thought crosses my mind, "What do you think of Truck?"

Birdie stands up and walks to me, instantly rubbing against my legs.

Interesting. I want to rub myself all over Truck, too.

I walk into the hallway and the smell of food makes my stomach rumble. Is he actually cooking for me? I knock on his door.

"One second," Truck yells through the door. The door opens and he speaks quicker than his normal patter as he runs back to his kitchen, "Come on in. Dinner is almost ready."

I close the door and inhale the delicious aroma of steak, but see him tending to a pot of pasta and a frying pan. There's a tinge of smoke in the air, he yells, "Shit. Shit. Shit." He pulls a pan from the broiler and plops it down on the cook top.

Something about the whole scene of this sexy, confident man cooking for me and not being absolutely perfect for a change is intoxicating. Stop right there. Don't get all girl-brained. Is he cooking for me or is he just cooking dinner? Stop making assumptions. He's put together wearing a fitted burgundy t-shirt and snug jeans. He even did something with his hair to take control and not let it run wild. Hot surfer to sin on a stick. I'd never complain about either.

His apartment is bigger than mine. The living room and kitchen area is wider. He has a room open to the living room with glass doors that's set up as his office. A few surfboards out on his balcony and a wetsuit hanging over the rail. The walls are all differing neutral shades of blue. I imagine the conversation with Vincent and the battle for more colors. This is the resulting compromise. The furniture is all modern and leather with dark wood accents. It's masculine, but not bach-elor pad. It's clean and everything has a place.

I hear a ping and Truck grabs his phone out of his pocket. He reads the message and turns toward me. His whole body relaxes in front of me as he smiles at me standing in the middle of his living room. He turns the burners off and walks over to me, "I didn't greet you very well. I need to fix that." He wraps his arm around my waist and lifts me until his lips meet mine ever so softly. He pulls back and gazes into my eyes while he sets me down, "I love this color on you." He turns to go back to the kitchen and stops. He reaches back for me and plants his hands on my cheeks, then leans down to kiss me. Full on, knock me on my ass, where the hell did that come from, kiss me until my knees give out, you're mine now, kiss me. I grab onto every part of him that I can in order to stay standing and he smiles against my lips. He lifts me up and I wrap my legs around his waist and my arms around his neck. When he takes his lips from mine, he grins from ear to ear, and doesn't put me down. He carries me to the kitchen and sets me down on the counter. "Stay in here with me while I finish up dinner?"

"Absolutely. Can I help with anything?" I ask and hope he says no since I'm useless in the kitchen and not sure I have the ability to stand.

"You can pour. What would you like to serve tonight, bartender?" He asks with a chuckle as he turns the burners back on.

"What goes with dinner, chef?" I ask.

He turns to me, "I can hold my own, but I'm no chef." He stops and continues, "Red wine is the match for spaghetti. Maybe we start with that and move to Jack after dinner?"

"I've had bad experience with wine and I don't like it," I scrunch my nose.

He hands me a bottle of lemon lime soda and a bottle of Jack, "About an inch of Jack and fill the glass with the soda. I think you'll love it and it won't over power dinner." He glances at me as I follow his instructions, "You had sangria at your housewarming party and that's wine with stuff added to it."

"Anything with liquor and fruit added is good. It doesn't even need the fruit," I laugh happily perched and unable to reach the floor. I observe as he goes back to cooking. He stirs tomatoes that have been cooking down to make a sauce and drops spaghetti into it a little at a time, getting all of the pasta coated. He uncovers a baking sheet with a huge steak on it and cuts it into thin slices. "What's the aroma making my tummy rumble," I ask.

"It's either the sauce with the cooked down onions, tomatoes, garlic, and peppers or the steak I rubbed with Italian seasoning, onion powder, and chili flakes."

Lucky steak. I'd like him to rub me.

He continues plating the pasta with slices of the steak on

top and grates thin pieces of parmesan over the top. "Couch or table?" He asks.

"Table please."

He nods and sets the plate on the table.

I'm still concerned my ass will hit the floor if my legs have not recovered. I scootch to the edge and reach for the ground, he laughs, "It's less than a foot." He grabs me around the waist and puts me safely on the floor. It happened quickly and I was happy to discover my stability had returned.

I take the one drink with me to find there's one huge plate to go with it. "One plate?" I ask.

"Family style," he smiles. "Don't you want to share with me?" He asks sincerely and I can only imagine the expression on my face that prompted him. He sets a smaller plate in front of me and at his place setting.

"Of course," I smile back at him and take a bite. "This is delicious. Have you been holding out on me?"

He laughs, "I've only got a few recipes in the arsenal. I sometimes mix and match."

"Whatever you did, thank you for inviting me to join you."

He stops and puts his fork down, "I'm sorry about every-thing. I wish you weren't getting evicted. I don't know what I was thinking the last ten days. If I ever do anything stupid like that again, please tell me. Don't let me be an ass."

"I'm only getting kicked out of my apartment, not disal-lowed from the building. We can still hang out. Maybe you can visit me at my new place sometime. If I ever find one."

"Maybe you just stay here," he says like it's an option.

"I love this building and I don't want to move. I've been searching for a new place since I got the notice and there's no place available that accepts pets and isn't infested with some-thing or outside of the zone Ashley will allow me to live in. She doesn't even have any acceptable vacancies in any of her buildings, which I would take at this point although I don't want her to be my landlord."

"I mean stay here."

"What part don't you understand? I'm being evicted! I don't have a choice! I can't stay here." I stop frustrated and start again, "And here I am being loud again. Next thing you know, you'll have an eviction notice for noisy guests."

"Will you listen to me?" He asks just as loud as I am. "Stay here. It will be fine."

"Vincent will have some crew come and move me if I don't move myself."

"Move in with me."

"What?"

"Move in with me."

"I can't. I'm blackballed as a bad person who disrupts the peace."

"That'll never happen again. Nobody will know you were evicted or moved in with me or any of it."

"Who are you kidding? This place has a secret rumor mill running through it named Cathy. They all know I'm the bad person and I have men over for sex."

"Then there's Vincent and his 'security cameras,'" he adds with air quotes.

"Oh, that's helpful."

"Move in with me. Try it for one week and we will see what happens. Just one week. Where else are you going to go?"

"Thanks for that. I could live in my car or go to Ashe's. I'm sure Birdie would love both of those. Did you forget I have a cat? You don't have pets. You'll have to get the cat pre-approved before I can move in."

"I'm telling you it won't be a problem. I kind of like Birdie."

"And your place isn't made for two people and a cat. You

are going to hate it having us confined here with you. Where would I even outlay stuff?"

"I'll make it bigger."

"You'll make it bigger? You're going to expand to the roof or something? You can't make an apartment bigger."

"I'll figure it out. There will be plenty of room."

I wonder if he's lost his marbles or if I'm just catching on to the fact that he's delusional.

"Raye, seriously. Don't look at me like I'm crazy. I can do this. Just give a week and try it."

Can it be worse than going back to crying Mac and early morning meeting Jonah? It does have its added benefits, well I assume it will have *benefits*. "Where will I sleep?"

He gives me a dirty grin, "With me. Will that work?"

"I'll try it," doing my best to be non-committal.

"Okay then. How about we finish dinner and you go pack up your personal items for a trial overnighter tonight?"

I nod and we quietly eat the rest of our dinner playing footsies under the table.

TWO DAYS LATER...

I've been staying at Truck's and moving things a little at a time as I can find room. When I get home from work, I'm going to figure out how he thinks he can make more room. I park and take the elevator up to the 4th floor. Before I can get down the hall I discover the door to my unit has been boarded up. "Fuck! I knew this wasn't going to work," tears spill from my eyes. I'm happy that Truck brought Birdie over to his place already.

Truck's door opens and he reaches for me, "What's wrong? Don't be upset."

"My door is boarded. I can't get in to get my stuff. I never should've let you talk me into this," I cry. "And I'm yelling again."

His arms go around me, "It's okay. I told you I would take care of it. Come with me." He leads me into his apartment and stands me in front of the empty space where there had been a wall between our apartments. "We don't need two kitchens, so I'm thinking we can turn one of them into a walk-in closet for you. It will be nice to have two and a half bathrooms and an extra bedroom. I was careful not to mess with Birdie's steps, so they're still there for her, too."

I stare at what he's done, "I'm so not getting my deposit back."

"Can you trust me on this? I've got it handled."

"How?"

"I've got a special connection with the owner. It's no problem."

"I don't have the money or the skills to repair this. This is the first time I've lived on my own. I've always had Ashe as my back-up. I'm surprised I've been able to keep Birdie and myself alive. I killed the plant I bought. I can't cook if it doesn't involve a microwave. I don't have a clue why you want me here."

He's frustrated with me and I've got him off kilter, "Stop. Just stop." He takes a deep breath, "I've never wanted anybody here. It's always been exactly what I wanted it to be all by myself. But you... you drive me crazy and I can't stop thinking about you and I can't have you living anywhere else. You need to be with me."

I smile at him, "You're not bad yourself, but that's not going to fix this living situation and the hole you made in the building."

"I own the building," he blurts out.

"What?"

159

"Vincent works for me. Nobody else in the building knows and I'd like to keep it that way."

"You own this building?"

"Yes and Vincent is going to raise everyone's rent to make up the difference of losing a unit."

"Is there anything else I should know?"

"I'm not a contractor. I just do the jobs around here that Vincent refuses to do."

"So you don't have a job where you work from home?"

"No, my office is where I do research and work on finding additional properties."

I want to ask him how many properties he has, but it's none of my business, so I stick with what I have a grasp on, "You some kind of sugar daddy?"

"No, just a panty thief."

EPILOGUE

SIX MONTHS LATER...

RAYE

*T*he only thing wrong with Truck is that he can't dance. He's got a fluid motion with no beat whatsoever and I love the way his hands are all over me. He wasn't a huge fan of the club at first, but he still takes me there to go dancing at least once every week. Again, he can't dance, but what he lacks in dancing skills he makes up for with effort and attitude. He also gets worked up on the dance floor, so it makes for a long enjoyable night after we get home. At first he didn't like the attention I got from the dogs at the club and I was concerned we were going to have the *how many* conversation–luckily, we didn't have to go there. I was especially concerned when one of them eyeballed him and asked, "How do you like my girl?" Though that wasn't as bad as the night Maddux walked into the club and stared at me for over twenty minutes, then tried to cut in. I always thought Maddux had a good body, but compared to Truck–he must've been drunk to even approach a man that much bigger than he is. Seriously, at least a half a foot taller and wider. He was an issue, too. Truck somehow recognized him and wanted to beat his ass. I handled the problem in my own way and managed to satisfy Truck and piss off Maddux at the same time, win-win for me. I kissed Truck hard and took advantage of the music to grind on him until he picked me up and carried me out of the place to have his way with me. I may have batted my eyes like Bambi and waved at Maddux as I was manhandled. Manhandled? Yea, that's a good thing. This man can pick me up and throw me around at his whim and I welcome it. His large strong man-hands, every time I see them all I can think about is the way they grasp my hips and dig into my flesh when he takes me. I have made some changes in compromise. We go to the club at 10pm instead of midnight, so we have longer for the after party. Is it still a compromise when it's self-satisfying? Besides, I don't need to walk in like a spectacle to get the attention of the dogs–I've got Truck.

Truck and everything that goes with him is something I was never interested in. I was content being a party girl on the prowl and accepting attention from a sugar daddy now and again, until I wasn't. I'm still confused about how it happened. I found an apartment, moved to the apartment, enjoyed a couple booty calls from my neighbor, got evicted, and moved in with my hottie neighbor to discover our apartments had become one. Over the last six months we've spent every night together and most of our free time. He's actually got me in the kitchen cooking with him, and I mean more than microwave popcorn. Get your head out of the gutter! We don't do that stuff in the kitchen. Well, only once.

TRUCK

My Raye of sunshine and I have adapted to living together. I take her to the club she loves and she goes to the beach with me. I've almost got her talked into learning how to surf. She's a sight sitting on the sand in her shorts and bikini top, with those huge sunglasses she loves to wear. What she wears to the club is a problem. If her ass or tits don't hang out of it, it doesn't qualify for the club. Then add her bouncing around on the dance floor. I'm not a club guy, but I'll be damned if my beautiful woman goes out without me. If I'm being straight about it, she drives me crazy on the dance floor and I'll never give up a second of it. The way she swings her hips and her overt confidence. I understand why she gets attention.

Which leads me to the nights with no sleep. I've got her panties off of her before we get home on club nights, if she's wearing any. I installed an extra layer of insulation and sound-proofing in our bedroom after the 3am noise complaints started coming in. Non-club nights we sleep, but only because we start earlier. Sometimes I like my dessert right after dinner.

Now, I look at my apartment six months later and every-thing has changed. It's not the place I eat, sleep, and store my surfboards. It's home. It's warmer than it used to be and more functional for all of us. We've customized the two apartments into one and it'll be a lot of work to put it back if I ever sell the building. But, that doesn't matter. What matters is Raye. She's home, or Truck's garage if you will. She makes me happy and keeps me satisfied. I think I do the same for her. I hope I do.

BIRDIE

The chin scratcher is in love with me. He took me from my apartment, doubled the size of my home, and invited my servant to live with us. He's made sure I have a place to sleep or perch in every room. He arranged outdoor access on the balcony. I even have my own room for private time with my sand box and my own faucet that produces water on my command. While I do so much enjoy his scent... he should never have allowed me to roam the hallway if he wanted me for himself. The old woman at the end of the hall often has her door open and I can't resist the aroma of her baked goods. I think she drugged me and on the long path home I made a new friend. He's got large paws and a luxurious fluffy tail to go with his long white hair. He made eyes at me and rudely sniffed my butt. I liked it. He's got a heavenly scent of tuna and catnip, I'm sure it's what keeps me going back to visit. Alas, all he wants to do is lie around and sleep. It horrifies me that he allows his servant to scratch his belly and stroke his tail. He has no dignity at all. I will not allow myself to be interested. Though, I'm afraid he has my attention and I mustn't allow him to degrade my stature in the feline kingdom. Maybe I will run laps in the hall later tonight and work him out of my system. I need to do something to maintain my svelte figure with all the treats I've been eating. For now, I will wander home and see if the chin scratcher or my servant have a free hand to rub behind my ears and help put me to sleep for my nap.

RAYE

It's been the longest work week in history. I'm tired and focused on getting home. I haven't talked to Ashe in a few days and our weekends have been busy.

Raye: Are you available?

Ashley: Getting ready to go to your place.

Raye: You're coming to my place?

My phone rings and I answer without a hello, "You're coming over tonight?"

"Yea, you didn't know?"

"Nope," then again I'm wasted this week and maybe I don't remember.

"Interesting."

"How is that interesting? Why are you coming over?" I stop and correct quickly, "I mean I want to see you. Seems like it's been weeks or maybe that's just how long my week has been. When did weeks start feeling like 15 days?"

"Rattling on. Never a good sign. Truck called. We are coming over for dinner. Something about too much tri-tip and donut holes."

"Huh," sounds like Trucks version of a fancy dinner with dessert.

"What am I missing here?"

"Truck only shares donut holes on special occasions or when he's consoling someone."

"Are you saying I may be underdressed?"

I chuckle at my always over-thinking bestie, "You are fine."

"You don't know what I'm wearing."

"I don't need to. As long as you aren't naked it will be acceptable." I continue because sometimes I can't help myself, "Naked would be fine, too. Except nobody wants to see all the baby fat and stretch marks."

"Thanks for that."

"Any time."

"I'm thinking about what you said. Tired? How tired? Do you have insomnia? Have you been up all night having sex?"

"We've been limiting the all-nighters to two per week. I can't fake functioning at work if we go more than that."

"How are you feeling?"

I thought I was clear, "Tired?"

"I meant overall. Any vomiting or nausea? Sensitivities to smells?"

Are we doing this again? "Ashe, you can hope that I'm pregnant all you want. There's no way that can happen."

"There's always a way," she says confidently.

"Not with my fortress."

"The only thing that's 100% is abstinence and that is not you."

"I'm aware of that. I use a combination of things to have a backup. I'm not pregnant."

"You could be pregnant. Have you taken a test?"

"Why would I take a pregnancy test? I'm not pregnant and I don't have any symptoms."

"You said you're tired."

"You're tired, too. Are you pregnant?" I ask flippantly.

Silence.

I change my tone, "Ashe, are you pregnant?"

"Can you please not ask me that question?"

"No problem."

"Good. Now, are you late?"

"No, I'm on track to be home at my normal time."

"That's not what I meant."

"Oh! I don't know. I don't keep track of that."

"Check your pills."

"I'm driving and there's no reason to bother with this."

"Have you broken any condoms?"

We did break two that one night after the club last month. "Well, you know they don't make them the way they used to."

"So, that's a yes. And you're still humping like bunnies? It wasn't like a quickie honeymoon phase and now it's over?"

"Every night. I love that man's tongue and cock," I say out loud unintentionally.

"Thanks for that. Didn't you have an ear infection last month?"

"Yeah, I still don't know where that came from. The antibiotics knocked me on my ass."

"Yep. You're pregnant."

"I'm not pregnant."

"Antibiotics make the pill useless. So, were the antibiotics before the broken condom or after?"

"Fuck me. Why didn't you tell me that before? I could've wrapped my body in plastic wrap or got a chastity belt or moved in at your place for a couple weeks or made him double up—no triple up on the condoms."

"Are you saying it's possible?"

"You said it, not me."

"Tossing a test in my bag for you now. I don't know why though, I'm pretty sure you're pregnant."

"All of this because I'm tired?"

"It's a slippery slope my friend."

"Very slippery and my friend is off her rocker."

"It's your life, not mine. I'd just rather know sooner than later."

"There's nothing to know."

"I'll just leave the test with you in case you want it."

"No. I don't need that and I don't want it anywhere around Truck."

"Fine. See you in an hour."

"Okay, can't wait to see you…" she hung up before I could finish. Why do I let her do this to me and get in my head? I pull into the next parking lot and dig my pills out to check. I should be starting today. No wonder I'm tired. I drive home relieved.

TRUCK

I invited Ashley and Jonah to join us for dinner tonight. Dinner is coming along well. I've got tri-tip resting, baked potatoes ready to come out of the oven, broccoli ready to steam in the microwave at the last minute, cheese sauce thickening on the cooktop, and Jodi dropped off a box of various donut holes for me about an hour ago. I've got options of ice cream, cool whip or canned whipped cream for dipping the donuts, and Hawaiian rolls to go with dinner because everything is better with Hawaiian rolls. I've got champagne chilling in the refrigerator.

The doorbell rings and Raye isn't home yet. I yell toward the door, "Come on in!"

In walks Ashley followed by Jonah, "Hello! It's so nice to be out for some adult time. Thank you for inviting us over."

Jonah reaches out to shake hands, "How are you doing?"

I stare at Jonah and keep my cool, "Never better. Dinner is about ready, but Raye isn't home yet."

Ashley gazes around, "You've done more since the last time I was here. Are you one of those that thinks things are never done?"

"No. I'd rather be done, but not until it's everything I want for me and Raye."

"Did you knock out more of the wall that was between the units?"

"I left it because it's got Birdie's steps on the other side, but I moved the whole wall over to make the main living room bigger, covered where the door was, and added a storage closet."

Birdie bumps against my leg and I bend down to scratch her chin.

"It looks great," she grins. "Are you going to paint?"

"No. She likes her goldfish and orange pillows and stuff.

Besides, I don't want to deal with Vincent. It's just not worth it. We may have him put in a mosaic backsplash in the kitchen. Raye liked the sun. I'm hoping for something more water themed." I take a deep breath.

"Tell Vincent when you hire him for the job," Jonah suggests.

"That's not how this works. The artiste will be moved to do something in the room. I will pay for it and he will do it on work time," I think about the cost of removing his artistic installations.

"But you're the boss."

"I think I gave up that position years ago," I chuckle at the truth of it all. It's worth it if I never have to replace Vincent.

Ashley chimes in, "I get it. It's important to choose your battles and understand the value of people."

Of course she would get it. She's a property manager. I smile at her happy to have someone around who gets it. I need her on my side. So far everything is going as planned. Raye is the wild card. I've got a decent read on her most of the time now, but sometimes she still surprises me with her reaction. Hmmm, she should be home by now.

Truck: Everything okay?
Raye: Yep. Needed to make a stop on the way home.
Truck: Ashley and Jonah are here for dinner.
Raye: Already?
Truck: Yep. No rush.
Raye: I won't be long.
Truck: 🤍

"She's on her way," I announce. "I need to finish up dinner. Feel free to make yourselves at home and help yourself to whatever you'd like to drink." Ashley follows me to the kitchen for drinks. I hit the start button on the microwave, set the plates out on the counter, and grab the champagne flutes from the top shelf.

"Ooooh, champagne. Fancy," Ashley coos.

"Raye likes the bubbles," I smile at the thought.

Ashley stops and leans on the kitchen counter with her feet crossed, "You really like my girl, don't you?"

"I suppose I do," I say with a one-sided shrug.

"If you hurt her, I'll beat you," she says sincerely.

"You have nothing to worry about."

She nods and goes to Jonah with two glasses in hand, "Everything smells so good."

"Thank you," I say as the door opens and Raye walks in. I gaze at her happy she's home, but something is off. Not good for my plan. "I've got dinner ready, are you hungry?"

"Give me a minute," she says and disappears into the other room with bags in her hands.

I go after her and wrap my arms around her, turning her to me to give her a quick kiss.

"What's gotten into you?" She asks.

"Am I not allowed to kiss my woman?" I ask smugly.

Her attitude changes, and she smiles, "I'm not complaining."

"Good. I'm going to plate dinner," I turn to leave the room.

"Why'd you invite Ashe over?"

"She's like your sister and I hardly know her. I've only met Jonah once."

"Oh, Ashe is in charge."

"I know. Of everything," I grin and leave the room.

I've got the table set for four. I slice the tri-tip and lay it out on each plate. Cut into the potatoes and squeeze them from the ends to open them up so they show their fluffy interior. Grab the broccoli from the microwave and toss it around with the herbs and butter I steamed it with. Two rolls on each plate because you can't eat just one. I put a softened stick of butter on a plate and place it on the table along with the cheese sauce, salt, and pepper. I carry the plates two at time to the table, "Okay, dinner is ready." Jonah and Ashley move to the table, bringing their drinks with them.

"Raye?"

"Be there in a second," she calls back.

I grab the bottle from the refrigerator and the champagne flutes, so I have it ready when it's time.

Raye joins us at the table, obviously tired and has had enough of today already. I pat her thigh, "All we are doing tonight is eating and relaxing. I thought we'd let Ashley pick the movie."

She smiles and runs her hand down my arm affectionately before she takes a bite of dinner. Her day strips away from her as the conversation takes over and the food satisfies her belly.

I stand up and pop the cork on the champagne. "How about a toast?" I say as I pour. I pass a glass to Jonah and another Ashley. I turn away and reach into my pocket. This is the moment. It's not what I had originally planned, but I can't wait any longer. I drop the almost-a-carat round diamond platinum ring with clusters of small round diamonds on each side into her glass. I turn to face her and hand her the glass as I kneel down on one knee. I take her free hand—

I'm interrupted by Ashley, "Oh my god!" She squeals and Raye stares at her like she's lost her marbles. "Sorry, go on," she says calmly.

"Raye, I admit that I didn't want you to move into the building. I wanted nothing to do with you."

She opens her mouth ready to go off and Ashley reaches across the table smacking her on the arm, "Shush!"

I chuckle, "No matter how hard I tried, I couldn't stay away from you. The more I get to know you, the more I need you with me. I never wanted a roommate, and I wasn't inter-ested in a partner. You are so much more to me. My home. My everything. Raye, I know I've never said it, but I love you. I need you. Only you. Will you marry me?"

Ashley is nodding yes silently at a frantic pace while Raye stares at me. I'm missing something and suddenly worried she's going to say no. Ashley gets up quickly and grasps Raye's hand with the glass in it and swirls it in front of her face. Her eyes widen and her lips turn up as she drinks the champagne. She takes the ring in her fingers and hands it back to me, "Try again."

I grin and slide the ring onto her left ring finger, "Raye, anything and everything for you always. Please be my wife."

Her lips twitching like she's trying to hold it in, "YES!" She leans in and kisses me. "Love? Is that what this is?"

I gaze at her, "I think so, I've never experienced it before. I just know I only want you."

"I love you, Truck."

THREE YEARS LATER...

RAYE

"I'm only getting pregnant this third time for you, so take the test already," Ashley says sternly as we stand in my bathroom together with pregnancy tests.

"You first," I reply not sure I want to be pregnant again when Sunshine is only two years old. I lean out of the room to check on Sunshine in her crib with Birdie napping next to her on babysitting duty. I turn to Ashe realizing what she said, "You are getting pregnant for me?"

"You don't want to go through the process by yourself, do you?"

"I'm sure I can handle it and you already have two," I glare at her.

"Humor me," she declares without any waver.

"Fine, same time and we set one timer?"

"Okay," she agrees and I run to the other bathroom to pee on the stick, quickly returning and locking us both in the bathroom together while Ashe sets the timer.

"This is the longest three minutes ever," I say.

"It's better to do something else and not think about it. Otherwise you'll be questioning what you want and if it's a boy or a girl and what you will name it. It's never-ending," she states obviously having more experience with this than me.

Interesting, "Do you want a third one? You already have Mac and Gin."

Ashe gives me a hard glare, "It's a bit late to be having that conversation."

"If it's a boy, I think I'll name it Gage. Trucks have gauges just like there's rays of sunshine."

"That's it?"

"Yep."

"What if it's a girl? Or twins?"

"I'll figure it out, but right now I want to dance," I hip bump my sister from another mister and raise my hands in the air as I sing an old dance club hit.

"Seriously?" Ashe asks.

"Why not?" I get my groove on.

"Is it three minutes yet?" She asks.

"You set the timer."

We both check the timer and watch as the alarm goes off.

"You know we didn't think this through very well," I say reflecting on the plan.

"What do you mean? We made a plan. I always have a plan," Ashley states confidently.

"If we are pregnant at the same time how are we going to take care of each other and help with the new babies?"

"That's what Jonah and Truck are for," she grins and we check the results. Two lines times two.

The door slams and the guys are back from surfing. "I'm home," Truck calls out.

I raise my eyebrows at Ashe, "Shall we handle this now and do it together?"

She pinches her eyes closed and I grab her hand dragging her to the living room. All three of our guys standing there shirtless with saltwater-tousled hair. I gaze at Ashe and tears are building in her eyes as her smile grows.

"Let's do it," I say hushed and squeeze her hand.

"We're pregnant!" We both exclaim.

Mac's eyes get big, "Another sister?" He asks almost worried about the number of girls in the house.

Ashe squats down to his level, "We don't know that yet. Could be a sister. Could be a brother."

Jonah wraps his arms around Ashe and Mac, "A new brother or sister either one will be wonderful." He winks at Ashe and kisses her cheek.

Truck stands across the room gazing at me. He slowly walks toward me and places his hands on my face. He leans down and brushes his lips against mine, worshipping my lower lip. Heated he says, "Two is a good number."

"I'd say it's the maximum number," I chuckle.

"Unless it's twins," Ashe chimes in.

"Shush!" I yell at her.

Truck leans his forehead against mine, "I never wanted any of it and now I want all of it."

"What if you have three girls in the house?" I ask.

"Girls can surf." He turns to Mac, "Isn't that right? We can take the girls surfing."

Mac nods enthusiastically. "Girls will be okay."

Ashe leans on Jonah observing, "My little nut."

Truck turns back to me with his full attention, "Are you ready to do this again?"

"I'm ready to do anything with you."

He picks me up and claims my mouth with his, carrying me to our bedroom. I wave over his shoulder, "Lock the door on your way out please." He sets me on the bed and skims up my thighs with his rough hands. Finding his way up my shorts he hooks his fingers around my string bikinis, but just when I think he's going to rip them off of me, he lets go. He unbuttons my shorts and pushes them off, leaving them hanging on my ankles. He buries his nose in my silky panties, rubbing against me and biting at me through the panties until he rips them away. His hands grasp my hips while he plays with me, teases me with his tongue. He's learned my combination and will make me wait until he's ready. But I can't wait and I grab onto him by the hair and buck at his face wanting more until he give its to me and I'm lost.

He flips me over and shoves into me from behind, taking me the way only he can. I come again and he goes with me, collapsing on the bed next to me. My Truck.

BIRDIE

It's nice to have someone to nap with. I'm getting used to the little being and trying to train her appropriately. Though my servant may have tricked me into assisting her. I suppose we all take care of family. I'm beginning to wonder if they understand how this happens, at least they have small litters. This place isn't big enough for many more. So far it's gone well, she's delicate when she touches me and only pulled my tail once—which I'm writing off as an accident. She does have an adorable little nose. I licked it once. The peeing in your bed thing is not dignified and I plan to teach her to use the box as soon as she is able to get on all fours. For now, I'll continue to help look after her—we all know the servant is challenged and the little being will have a better chance with me at the helm.

WHERE ARE THEY NOW?

VINCENT...

gave up fighting off the younger man and hired him as his property management assistant so he could open his own gallery and spend more time with his artwork. Truck agreed since he bought another building for Vincent to manage. But Vincent insisted that he move Joseph next door to him and connect the apartments at no cost and no rent... two buildings = two apartments.

JOSEPH...

is enjoying his new assistant duties as he would do anything for the amazing Vincent. He's happy living with him and having something to do. He thought he'd enjoy not working and quit when he hit it big on the lottery.

CATHY...

bought a hamster and keeps adding to its habit trail. She took advantage of Vincent to mount it on the wall and paint a mural around it. She loves his little beady eyes and lets him roll around the house in a ball. And enjoys watching Vincent paint even though he doesn't allow her to talk because it "disrupts his flow."

AGNES...

finally revealed that she's retired renowned baker Juliette Agnes Le Champ, founder and recipe creator of the famed Le Chomp Cookies. Vincent raised her rent by a dozen cookies per week.

MARY & HARRY...

are one notice away from getting evicted. They discovered KinksRUs offers a panty subscription service and have been enjoying the variety of backless, crotchless, and see-thru panties. The real trouble started when they received a free gift with their order, now they are using up batteries like crazy.

MADDUX...

continues to go to the fancy pants restaurant alone, always ordering the chef's menu with wine pairing. Nobody there will dance with him. He's losing his hair and in search of a new (younger) maid.

After many attempts to find companionship at the club and being robbed by a couple of the women he brought home, he changed his plan and signed up for a college class in search of younger women. He paid tuition for a few and started to date a couple of their mothers–who were friends and realized he was cheating on them with each other.

JONAH...

has been enjoying the job with Mighty Midge as his assistant. The company has given him raises making it hard to leave. He keeps saving the money and is taking the time to enjoy his family while he can.

ASHLEY...

never changes. She's still in charge of everything.

MAC...

spends half of each day at preschool and the other half of the day at the beach. His mom is making him take swimming lessons, so he can handle the waves when he goes surfing. He wants to go to this place the surfers talk about called Hawaii and his mom says he's already been there.

MARTA...

stuck with Mr. Quijada, watching the women come and go. He proposed to her and she declined saying that she's been in a committed relationship with the neighbor for years and he had his chance.

MUFFIN MAN

ROBBI

"Everybody out!" The manager yells, running through the salon as we all ignore her. She's not the owner. Problem is the owner is out of town and she's in charge. She stops and at the top of her lungs, "Evacuate now! It's going to explode!"

The salon freezes instantly, the calm before the storm. There's a sudden frenzy of women gathering their necessities, and their clients as they run outside hysterically. I casually get up out of the salon chair and walk out with Deanna, my stylist, close behind me, and avoid the trampling stampede of frantic, high-pitched women.

We all gather outside for the details, but the manager is still in there! She comes running out with the massage therapists and their clients wrapped in robes. It triggers me to survey the scene for what stages of beautification we're all in. I mean, we all go to the salon for different things. Personally, it's how I stay blonde and that's not changing any time soon because I can prove blondes have more fun. The stylists are brushing out their hair, fixing their make-up, taking off aprons. I overhear what's happening and empathize for some of the poor women in the middle of getting services, when it hits me—I'm one of them.

The building had started to make a banging noise. The manager, Shawna, had taken it upon herself to find the problem. She was left in charge after all and the ship was not going to sink under her direction. This isn't some basic barbershop, this is Michelle's Salon and Shawna would not be responsible for damage to the custom European style decor Michelle has taken years to refine. It was the water heater. The water heater was making the loud noise, like it had air in the line or was trying to pass bad Chinese food. It was also emitting gas fumes and sparked every time there was a bang. The bangs were getting more frequent.

Which brings us to the bunch of women now standing outside in the shade of the building's front awning. It's almost lunchtime and the parking lot of the strip mall is starting to fill up with patrons to the food establishments, eyes peering at the motley crowd of women in smocks milling around helplessly. Shawna's on the phone with 911 trying to get, yes, you guessed it, the fire department.

911: What's your emergency?
Shawna: There's going to be a fire
911: Is there a fire now?
Shawna: No, not yet.
911: Sorry, we can't help you yet
click

At least, that's how I imagine it from the story Shawna told. There were others calling, it would be fine. Help would show up. Hopefully. Deanna, the only person I will let near my hair, is getting fidgety and twirling her soft brunette curls between her fingers. "I'm sure they'll be here quick. We still have ten minutes before we have to wash the bleach out of your hair. Everything will be fine." For those of you who are not salon savvy, leaving chemicals on your hair too long isn't good. Hair will break off, fall out, burn. I've seen it smoke. All kinds of horrible things, and I take pride in my long platinum blonde hair. So, let me translate what Deanna said: Ten minutes until utter disaster. Others have half a haircut, shampoo or conditioner in their hair, extensions partially tied in. The people who were getting massages are relaxed, even if their clothes are inside the building and they're outside wearing only a robe.

Everyone that could primp, had primped for the firemen to show up. It's a lineup and I can imagine the firemen walking the line, *"I'll take this one, and this one. You don't mind sharing, right?"* The senior firefighter steps up and says, *"Sorry, I get first choice. Seniority gets perks. I'll be taking this one from you."* Anyway, you get the idea. It's a beauty pageant and then there's me with a plastic bag on my head and a lady with foils sticking up off her head like she could receive radio transmission.

The sound of sirens fill the air as the long red ladder truck pulls into the parking lot, stopping in front of the salon. The important thing here is the possible fire, but I appreciate firemen as much as the next girl, maybe more. Definitely more. I love a hot guy, even on days like today when I only get to drool from a distance because I look like a bag lady compared to the stylists. The first guy is a bit older with short salt and pepper hair. He's fit and fills his navy blue uniform nicely. The second guy is shorter, still at least 5'9" and wearing one of those bulky yellow jackets with reflectors. His face is adorable, but the jacket hides everything else—not a hint of a single ab or muscular arm. The third reminds me of Goldilocks, he's just right. Thick, dirty blonde hair and the mustache to match. His navy blue uniform pants are topped with his station T-shirt which stretches across his chest and shoulders, yet loose where it's tucked into his Dickies. I'm busy imagining the things I could do to him. Naked. With my tongue. Deanna stomps her boots and drags me into the dog groomer next door.

"Firemen? Hot firemen?" I whined questioningly, not wanting to give up my view.

Want more Muffin Man?
Get the book at naomispringthorp.com!

ACKNOWLEDGMENTS

Thank you to Symphony Publishing Press for allowing me to include "Pluckie" and its story reference from The Laundry List by the incomparable Rayne Elizabeth in The Panty Thief. No goldfish were harmed or in anyone's mouth during the writing of this book. You can find The Laundry List in Imperfect Date, A Romantic Comedy Collection.

Thank you to my sister from another mister for being by my side and supporting me when I need it and when I don't.

NAOMI SPRINGTHORP

USA Today Bestselling Author Naomi Springthorp is a born and raised Southern California girl who believes that life has a soundtrack and half of each year should be spent cheering for her favorite baseball team. She loves music and spending time with her feline fur babies.

Naomi writes Baseball Romance, Romantic Comedies, Contemporary Romance, and 90s Throwbacks—all with heat and sometimes a little sweet.

Sign-up for Naomi's newsletter at
www.naomispringthorp.com/sign-up
to get updates on everything she has going on.

Join Naomi's reader group Naomi's Naughties at
https://facebook.com/groups/naomisreaders
for fun, baseball, and hotties.

facebook.com/naomithewriter

twitter.com/naomithewriter

instagram.com/naomispringthorp

amazon.com/author/naomispringthorp

bookbub.com/authors/naomi-springthorp

goodreads.com/naomithewriter

tiktok.com/@naomispringthorp

pinterest.com/naomispringthorp

ALSO BY NAOMI SPRINGTHORP

AN ALL ABOUT THE DIAMOND ROMANCE

The Sweet Spot

King of Diamonds

Diamonds in Paradise (a novella)

Star-Crossed in the Outfield

The Closer (a novella)

Falling For Prince (A Short Stop)

Up to Bat

BETTING ON LOVE

Just a California Girl

Jacks

NOVELLAS AND STANDALONE NOVELS

Muffin Man (a novella)

Finally in Focus (a novella)

Confessions of an Online Junkie

ANTHOLOGIES & BOX SETS

Sacrifice for Love

Storybook Pub

Storybook Pub Christmas Wishes

Storybook Pub 2

Young Crush

Hate to Want You

Tricks, Treats, & Teasers

Caught Under the Mistletoe

Game On

Imperfect Date

www.ingramcontent.com/pod-product-compliance
Lightning Source LLC
Chambersburg PA
CBHW022152240626
47153CB00007B/2631